N. T. (Nathaniel Tuthill) Hubbard

Autobiography of N.T. Hubbard

With personal Reminiscences of New York City from 1789 to 1875

N. T. (Nathaniel Tuthill) Hubbard

Autobiography of N.T. Hubbard

With personal Reminiscences of New York City from 1789 to 1875

ISBN/EAN: 9783337120474

Printed in Europe, USA, Canada, Australia, Japan

Cover: Foto ©Raphael Reischuk / pixelio.de

More available books at **www.hansebooks.com**

AUTOBIOGRAPHY

OF

N. T. HUBBARD

WITH

PERSONAL REMINISCENCES

OF

NEW YORK CITY

From 1798 to 1875.

———◆———

NEW YORK:

JOHN F. TROW & SON,

205–213 EAST TWELFTH STREET.

1875.

DEDICATION.

To Col. Isaac H. Reed.

MY DEAR SIR:

It is with unfeigned pleasure I dedicate (with your permission) this little work to you, Sir, with whom I have been so long and so pleasantly associated, with so many pleasing incidents occurring in our intercourse, that it is indeed a pleasure and a pride to me to dedicate to you my book; and if it will while away a leisure hour, and call to your remembrance one who has the highest esteem and regard for you, it will indeed repay me.

Wishing you, my dear friend, many and prosperous days, I am

Truly and faithfully yours,

N. T. HUBBARD.

N. T. Hubbard

PREFACE.

HAVING had for several months past much leisure time on my hands, the thought occurred to me, early last Spring, that I could not improve my leisure hours better or to more advantage than to jot down a few reminiscences and recollections of the time, long gone by, in connection with a brief history of my early life. In these papers I have alluded quite often to my progenitors and many of my relatives, and I beg here to say—the remarks which I have made concerning them, were intended more particularly for them alone, than for the public generally. I have several times, during the writing of these papers, threatened to destroy what I had written, feeling as I frequently have, that I could not give that expression to my thoughts in language that altogether pleased me; but I was prevailed upon to go on, and I now present to my relatives and friends a little work which has taken me many months to complete, and which I sincerely trust may prove of some interest to my readers.

At my time of life (I am now in my ninetieth year) it can hardly be expected that I should possess the qualifications necessary to give to these papers anything approaching literary merit. This I certainly have not aspired to, but simply to relate in my own language and in my own way, some of the events which have occurred in this city during the past seventy-five or eighty years, and if I have contributed even in a small degree, any gratification or amusement to my readers, I shall be satisfied. Having lived far beyond the time allotted to man, and with a due sense of His great mercies to me—sparing me in my old age, and placing my trust still in Him, I await His summons, and may His blessings descend upon one and all of you.

N. T. HUBBARD.

INTERLUDE.

I am scribbling out in my old age (nearly ninety) some reminiscences of my own life, together with some historic facts of New York City, in which I have now resided seventy-six years; my memory at times is at fault and not so good as it was fifty years ago, so when a circumstance or an idea flashes on my mind of earlier recollections, I note it down, without regard to what I have previously written, therefore many of these pages will be somewhat disjointed. I have no apology to make on this account, as my own relatives and friends will not criticise the many inaccuracies these sketches contain. I have never traveled abroad, and know nothing of the great European cities beyond what I have read; but I feel myself pretty well posted, probably as much so as many tourists who have, from time to time, visited the European capitals. I have read for many years historic accounts from every portion of the globe. My travels in my own country have also been very limited.

The main portion of my life I have devoted to business in New York, and this, together with the superintendence of my large family, and the education of my children, in which I spared no expense, has occupied most of my time.

CONTENTS.

REMINISCENCES.

CHAPTER I.

MY EARLY LIFE.

I was born at Mattituck, Suffolk County, Long Island, on the 29th of May, 1785. I moved to New York with my father's family in 1798, and have resided here ever since. In very early life I was taken by a maiden aunt to my grandfather's, who lived adjacent to my father's. She had been betrothed, in early life, to a very excellent young man, who suddenly died; and my Aunt Mary would never after listen to any proposal of marriage. So she took me, a baby, for her idol; for she al-

1

ways loved and worshipped me to idolatry. A few years later, my father removed with his family to Blooming Grove, Orange County, leaving me with my aunt and grandfather's family. Some eight or nine years after, both of my grandparents died; then my father returned to Long Island and made arrangements to take me home with him; but my Aunt Mary insisted upon accompanying me, to which my father readily assented. She remained at my father's until the following spring, when she returned to Long Island, with a promise from him that I should be permitted to visit her once a year as long as she lived. He kept this promise for two years—he then sold out his property in Orange County and removed to New York in the fall of 1798—after this she visited my father's family in New York, and I regularly visited her every year to the end of her life. No son ever loved or worshipped his mother more sincerely than I did this excellent

and devoted aunt, and after her death
I caused a marble headstone to be placed
at her grave at Mattituck, Long Island,
where she was born and died. I was
employed for several years in the winter
with my uncle, Daniel Hubbard, who was
an inspector of provisions. During the
spring and summer I was frequently out of
employment, but having attained to my
majority (twenty-one years), I felt myself
capable of filling most any position that
might offer. At this time a proposal was
made (which I accepted), to take charge
of a school at East Hempstead, Long Island.
I remained there six months—at the end of
that time I returned to the city, and obtained employment for a year in the office
of James Roosevelt, sugar baker, in Pearl
Street, at a salary of $400 a year. I spent
the following summer with my uncle, Au-
gustus Griffin, who kept a retail store at
Oysterponds (now called Orient), on Long
Island. I was employed by him in writ-

ing up his books, and otherwise assisting him in the store.   In the fall I returned to the City, and was book-keeper for my uncle, Daniel Hubbard.

Shortly after I formed a copartnership with Mr. Samuel Fanning, who was also born on Long Island, under the firm name of Fanning and Hubbard, and we opened a grocery store in Catherine Street, opposite the market, between Cherry and Water Streets.   At the end of a year we dissolved partnership.   I continued in the grocery business for ten years, having removed to other locations in the meantime.   The last two years I was in this business I did not make my expenses by $1,500.   Business at this time not looking very bright, I called in an auctioneer, sold out my stock of goods, and (as previously arranged) I went down town and hired an office in Water Street, engaged a clerk at $30 per month, and enter-ed into the produce brokerage business, and soon procured a good set of customers, and in six months I earned sufficient to pay off the $1,500 I was in debt, besides supporting my growing family. From this time forward fortune favored me, and in the course of ten years I did a large commission business, and could advance from $50,000 to $100,000 in cash if required.

I was married in 1811 to Susan Logan, daughter of Major Samuel Logan, of Revolutionary memory, at New Windsor, Orange County. We lived together fifty-six years in perfect peace and harmony, she a true and devoted wife and mother—the idol of my younger days, and the prop and stay of my declining years. She died February 4th, 1867, in the eighty-second year of her age. We had five sons and five daughters, who lived to be over twenty-one years of age before I lost any of them by death. I have now four daughters and two sons living.

It may be of some interest to those who may read my little book to know something of the early history of New York. In 1798 the population of the city was about seventy thousand. At this time there were no buildings in Broadway above Chambers Street, except scattering ones, and there were not sixty houses in all Brooklyn, from the Navy Yard to the South Ferry. We then crossed to Brooklyn in small-boats. The fare was 6d. Some years after, a horse-boat conveyed passengers across the river.

The first steamboat was built by a Mr. Brown, on the East River, some five or six blocks above Rutgers Street, under the direction and supervision of Robert Fulton, some sixty-five or seventy years ago. I was then a clerk with my uncle at Corlear's Hook, and passed the yard in which it was being built twice a day. My father then resided in Henry Street. I frequently stopped and went on board of her while in progress of building. I likewise saw her start on her first and trial trip to Albany.

In speaking of New York, I would here remark that the old inhabitants have all passed away, but I well remember many of the prominent merchants of sixty-five and seventy years ago. Daniel Lydig, John B. Cole, Suydam & Wykoff, and John Townsend. Among the largest shipping merchants were Leroy, Bayard & McEvers, Archibald Gracie, Robert Lenox, Minturn & Champlin, and many others whom I have forgotten. At a later date Isaac Wright & Son established the first regular line of packets between this port and Liverpool, known as the Black Ball line. This house was among the first to patronize me. When I first commenced the produce brokerage business I received regular orders from them to purchase from three hundred to five hundred bushels of rye, and supplied the beef and pork for stores for their ships. Jeremiah Thompson was also connected with them in this line of packets. For several years I monopolized the rye flour market, and bought up three-fourths of all that arrived here, and supplied all the jobbing flour dealers, together with the shippers. The old firm of Hay & Wood were the largest shippers of rye flour at this period.

I had a contract for one year, in connection with a reliable person who resided at Sing Sing, to supply the inmates of the prison, being the lowest bidder. I took the contract at nine cents per day for each prisoner. The prison fare consisted of rye flour, Indian meal, prime beef, prime pork, molasses, vinegar, salt, and dry codfish, rye for coffee, and occasionally beans and peas, together with potatoes. Of this latter article I purchased one day at New Slip fifteen hundred bushels at ten cents a bushel. At the termination of the contract we had made a little over $1,500.

Among the old prominent wholesale grocers of sixty years ago were Eldad Holmes, Stebbins & Couch, Peter G. Hart,

Stevens & Lippincott, Wardle & Wood, J. Johnson & Sons, Hopkins & Hawley, and many others too numerous to mention. The wholesale iron dealers were Pierson & Co., Francis Saltus & Co., and Blackwell & Co. Among the dry goods merchants I had little or no communication. I recollect the old silk house of Vandevoort & Flanden, in Broadway, and Lewis Tappan, in Pearl Street. We had no A. T. Stewart in those days; but, digressing a moment, I will here relate a little occurrence that took place in Tappan's store, shortly after Stewart opened his store on Broadway.

Tappan had just received a small invoice of silks, which he had imported. Among his other customers Mr. Stewart called and found a case of silk that pleased him, but he had not sufficient means on hand to pay for it. He bought the case, however, and paid down one-half the cost of it, and agreed to pay the balance in a day or two. He took from the case what he had paid for on account, and, agreeably to his engagement, called in a day or two and paid the balance due and took the remainder of the silk. This fact was related to me by Mr. Cyrus Chenery, my son-in-law.

MY ANCESTRY.

My mother's family was large. I was the eldest son, and the only one now living. My sisters and brothers all had families, so I must necessarily have many relatives scattered around the country, aside from my grandchildren and great grandchildren; and of those whom I have never seen I may only hope that their future in life may be attended with every success; and may that Almighty Power so guide and guard them that this result may be obtained.

In my prolonged life I necessarily have had great experience, and were it now in my power to speak to one and all of you

I should say, be honest and just to your fellow-men; never forgetting the great blessings your Heavenly Father has bestowed upon you; resign yourselves to His care, and He will never desert you.

In 1783 my father married Mary Tuthill, at Rocky Point, Long Island. Her father's name was Nathaniel Tuthill, by which name I was christened. He left very large landed estates to his widow, and it was currently reported and generally believed that she was the richest widow on Long Island. Her income was some $1,200 a year, which at that early period was equal to $12,000 a year at the present time. It was further reported of him that he was one of the best men that ever lived; he died early in life, mourned and regretted by every one who knew him. I have great reason to be proud and thankful that I sprung from such noble ancestry, who were so universally admired and loved to the close of their lives.

A STROLL IN CENTRAL PARK.

May 11th, yesterday, Sunday, I attended church on the corner of Fifth Avenue and Twenty-ninth Street—the Dutch Reformed. The Rev. Dr. Ormiston gave one of his most thrilling discourses on the subject of death. He stated in the course of his remarks that he had attended four funerals of his congregation during the week. He is a man of superior talent, and is a striking light among his brother-clergymen. From the church I took the cars and rode to Central Park; it was decidedly the warmest day we had yet had. After a short ramble in the Park I returned and made one or two visits. One to my old friend, Dr. Robinson, who has resided many years on the south side of Washington Square, whose age is within about four months of my own; he has been totally blind for several years past.

Dr. Robinson was born in this city, in

South Street, between Peck Slip and Roosevelt Street. He married a Miss Bull, who resided in Rutgers Street with her father, while my father's family resided two doors below. One of my sisters was very intimate with this lady. She died some twelve or thirteen years ago, and I was one of the pall-bearers at her funeral. She was a splendid and most accomplished lady. Captain Bull, the father of the Doctor's wife, was formerly an old sea-captain, but had retired from the service and had opened a lumber yard in Cherry just above Rutgers Street.

One day, during the war with Great Britain in 1812, Captain Bull had an application from one of our oldest and largest shipping-houses to make the voyage to China in one of their vessels, as both captain and supercargo, for which he was promptly offered $10,000 for the round voyage. After two or three days' reflection he accepted the offer, and the ship was immediately loaded and shortly after sailed. She made a prosperous voyage, and returned, about fifteen or sixteen months afterwards, safe and sound, escaping the numerous privateers scouring the ocean at that time.

During the war I was drafted for military duty in one of the forts in our harbor. I had been married the year previous, and besides I had my store to look after, and I felt very unwilling to leave both my family and business, so I applied to my only brother offering him my outfit and thirty dollars a month to go as my substitute, which he promptly accepted. I was then a member of a uniformed company of light artillery, composed of the most respectable young men of the city. Our captain was Henry Morgan, a wholesale grocer, then doing business corner of Peck Slip and Front Street. I never had any taste for military life, and invariably objected being elected from the ranks to any office, although repeatedly solicited, but I would nominate some one of my friends for the office intended for me, and of those very men I first nominated for a subordinate office was Colonel Hopkins, afterwards of the old firm of Hopkins & Hawley. He was shortly after elected General of the Brigade; he has been dead several years.

Among the more prominent shipping merchants whose acquaintance I made were Robert Lenox, who imported from Jamaica large quantities of rum, sugar and molasses; N. L. & G. Griswold, Boorman & Johnston, Joseph Foulk & Sons, G. G. & S. Howland, afterwards Howland & Aspinwall, Peter Stagg & Co., Alsop & Chauncey, David Lydig, Peter I. Nevius, Grinnell & Minturn, and many others whom I cannot at this moment call to mind.

GABRIEL HAVENS.

In some portion of these papers I have already spoken of the Havens family, but I find it necessary to enlarge on it in connection with others of my paternal ancestry, viz., Havens, Hallock, Hubbard and Tuthill. Gabriel Havens was own cousin to my grandmother, Mary Tuthill, whose maiden name was Havens. My grandfather married a Miss Hallock, while Mr. Hallock married a sister of grandfather Hubbard—the above formed my ancestry. All these families were from the most respectable citizens of Long Island, and their descendants to-day in point of respectability and influence will compare most favorably with those of any other in this country, as there is no blot or stain upon their names.

Gabriel and his brother Philetus were shipping merchants in this city seventy years ago. Gabriel Havens, at a later period of his life, was Harbor Master in this city for several years. Mr. Havens and wife were at my eldest daughter's wedding, as were also Mr. and Mrs. Crary. Mr. Crary married the youngest sister of Mr.

Havens, and there may be some of our older citizens now living who may remember the old firm of Peter and John Crary; the latter lived for many years opposite St. John's Park. Mr. Gabriel Havens died in this city some forty-five years ago. Mr. Chenery, my son-in-law, was a watcher at his bedside the night he died. There was a strong intimacy existing between the Rev. Dr. Spring and Mr. Havens' family, the latter having attended the church of Dr. Spring for many years. After the death of Mr. Havens, his body was removed by packet to Sag Harbor, and from thence to his father's private burying-ground. Dr. Spring accompanied the remains to their last resting-place, and performed all the services for his departed friend.

CHAPTER II.

MY FIRST SCHOOL.

At about the age of five years I was first sent to school. A widow lady by the name of Chase presided over this institution. She resided within a half mile of my grandparents, and being of a kind, motherly disposition, she very soon ingratiated herself into the good graces of all her scholars. I have but little to say regarding our mental improvement; suffice it to say, she was not exactly educated for a schoolmistress, but notwithstanding this she could repeat the alphabet, and this at times with some effect. I am joking over my old schoolmistress, but it was she who first taught me my A B C. Those happy schoolboy days!

At about this time we had "our clergyman" at Mattituck, who gloried in the
name of Goldsmith. He was a farmer. I
never knew who his spiritual teachers were;
possibly he may have been his own tutor.
He was at best a prosy old crone, and had
a disagreeable way of see-sawing his body
in the pulpit while speaking. Our little
church was located in the immediate vicinity of a tavern, and before our learned
friend ascended his pulpit he invariably
partook at this tavern of his favorite beverage, which consisted of a mixture of sugar
and gin. My recollections of this individual
are somewhat vague, but there is a character in one of Dickens's works, a lawyer (if
I mistake not, in "Oliver Twist"), who is
the counterpart of what this learned divine
once was.

SIMONY, OUR SLAVE.

My grandmother Tuthill owned a slave
named Simony, which she gave to my

mother shortly after her marriage. This slave girl was a great favorite in my father's family. She was an uncommonly good-looking girl of the mulatto type. She was particularly fond of dress, and my mother humored her somewhat in this regard. We all became very much attached to her. My mother sent her to school as regularly, during the summer as she did her own children. When my father concluded to remove to New York, she became very uneasy and discontented, and begged that my mother would find a new master for her and sell her, as she did not wish to go to New York. My mother knew the reason why Simony was so opposed to going with us to the city.

Previous to our removal to Orange County, she had formed an intimate acquaintance with a young colored man, on Long Island, of excellent character (a slave also), who, after my father's removal to Orange County, persuaded his master to

sell him to a rich farmer, who lived near
Goshen, Orange County, and the sale was
soon after effected—hence the reason why
Simony was so opposed to going with the
family to New York. When the young
man was installed in his new master's employ, he frequently visited Simony at our
home. Just previous to our leaving for
the city, my mother one morning ordered
her horse saddled, and told the family she
was going to Goshen on some important
business; and when she returned, in *the
afternoon, she told the family that she had
sold Simony to the master of her lover, and
that she would go to her new home in the
course of a week. There was crying and
rejoicing at the same time, for all the
children were devotedly attached to her.
In a short time after her advent in her new
home, Simony and her lover were married.
She did not live many years to enjoy her
married life, for she fell into a decline and
died within three years afterwards.

TRAINING DAY.

While yet a lad residing at my native place I remember the most prominent holiday of the year was the general training day, which usually occurred in May and invariably took place at Mattituck, my native place, where the men subject to military duty assembled from thirty miles distant. It was the custom in those early days for the women and girls to accompany the male members of the household on these occasions; in short, making it a general holiday for all. The whole scene was an enlivening one, and the grown portion of the company enjoyed themselves to the full. All kinds of sports were indulged in, and one happy day, at least, was passed amid enjoyments and in social intercourse. Old associations were renewed and new friendships formed. In fact, the day of all others in the year was Training Day.

CHAPTER III.

THE FISHERIES OF LONG ISLAND.

In my very early youth, I remember, in the spring of each year, the inhabitants of Long Island, from River Head to Oysterpond Point, engaged from four to six weeks in fishing for moss bunkers for the express purpose of manuring their lands. A number of the farmers would unite together and have a large seine manufactured, in which they all took shares, and when the fishing season arrived they would employ a number of men to man and manage one of these immense seines, which were placed on the beach and inlets in the bays between River Head and Oysterpond. Immense windlasses were erected on the beach to draw the seine when a

school of fish was discovered by the men.
These seines, on an average, would com-
pass a circle of two miles. There have
been numerous instances in which the
fishermen would watch day and night for
a week together without seeing a school;
then again they would come in with a perfect rush.

I recollect one day, with my father,
visiting my uncle Halleck; whose large
farm was about a mile south of Southold
Town, and where a large inlet extended
some three or four miles. On the beach
the fishermen had erected their shanties
and the large windlasses. On going down
to the beach that morning I beheld a sight
I can never forget—the whole beach for a
mile or more was literally covered with
the fish. It was estimated the haul of that
morning would reach two and a half
millions of moss bunkers. On this particular occasion many of the large land-
owners, who were shareholders, could not

find vehicles sufficient to remove their proportion of the haul. The lands in this neighborhood have been made rich by these fish productions, and I believe the same fisheries that prevailed eighty years ago are still carried on in a greater or less degree.

It is well known that Long Island Sound has long been noted in connection with fisheries for the immense number of porpoises it contains. I remember, when a boy, that some of our fishermen clubbed together and manufactured a seine for porpoise fishing, for the express purpose of obtaining the oil; it proved, however, a failure, and was abandoned after two or three years.

WHALE SHIPS.

What marvellous changes have occurred within the past sixty years! Thousands upon thousands have been born, and thousands upon thousands have died in that

2

period of time; thousands of wealthy and influential families have become impoverished, and thousands of poor have become wealthy; business has increased beyond all calculation—from a dozen brokers in produce fifty years ago, they can now be numbered by regiments, and still they come. During the early days of my brokerage life, I did a large business in supplying our fleet of whaling ships with beef and pork for their voyages out and home. In several of them I had an interest. When a new whaler was being built, the cost was put into shares of $250 each, to which, when requested by the agents, I subscribed from one to five shares. Some of them paid good dividends, while others were not so fortunate.

The fleet of whalers at present is reduced to a very small number; this fact is principally owing to the great increase of the petroleum productions of later years, which has proved a substitute

for whale oil, and is sold at such low
prices that the whaling interest is nearly
banished from the ocean. Twenty or
thirty years ago, on visiting the large
whaling ports down east, viz. : New Bedford, New London, Nantucket, Sag Harbor, and Greenport, the wharves were literally alive with business in discharging the
arrivals of whale ships, and the preparations in fitting-out and loading others for
their long voyages. Visit those places
now and you will find them almost utterly
deserted; instead of their former activity,
you will find their wharves fast going to
decay, and scarcely anything doing on
their former busy wharves. The few
whalers now on the ocean are on the track
for sperm whales, for a good cargo of
sperm oil would still pay a good profit
over the cost of obtaining it.

CHAPTER IV.

LONG ISLAND RAILROAD.

THE opening of the Long Island Railroad from Brooklyn to Greenpoint, many years ago, was quite an exciting affair. The president and directors of the company had invited their friends and the most prominent men of the island to meet the train at the different stations, and proceed on to the end of the road; hence our train was well packed by the time we reached Greenpoint, the end of our journey. I was one of the invited guests. The directors of the company had made ample provision to entertain all their guests, together with the numerous collection of people for miles around who had assembled to witness the arrival of the first train at

Greenpoint. The day was fine, and in a field near the depot a sumptuous repast was spread. It was truly an interesting occasion, for I then met many old acquantainces whom I had not seen for years. My old uncle Griffin was there to meet me, and after the close of the entertainment I returned with him to his home in Orient, some six miles east of Greenpoint, and spent the night with him, and returned to New York the following day.

I will here give a little history of Mr. Griffin. He married my mother's sister, and was altogether one of the most agreeable and pleasant men I ever knew; he was most excellent company for either young or old. He died a few months before he completed his hundredth year. In early life he was a school teacher, after relinquishing which he opened a country store in Orient (then called Oysterponds), which he continued for many years. During a long period of his life he kept a diary,

in which he collected and recorded many
interesting incidents, but more particularly the history of all the earlier set-
tlers on the eastern shores of Long Isl
and. When about ninety years of age,
agreeably to his previous intention, he, with
his only son, a lawyer by profession, took
up his old diary and collected therefrom all
the most important incidents it contained,
and prepared the same for publication,
which was duly printed in 1857, under the
title of "Griffin's Journal." It covers a little over three hundred pages. I subscribed
for twenty-five copies, and the only copy
remaining in my possession is now before
me; the remainder I have given away to my
friends as they wanted them, and during
the past two or three years I have received several letters from parties residing in
the West, requesting me to advise them if
I knew where copies could be obtained.
My impression is, the edition is entirely ex-
hausted. The dedication of this book was,

"To my son, Sidney L. Griffin, and good friend,
Nathaniel T. Hubbard, Esq."

I herewith copy one extract of his life, as given by himself in his own brief history as follows: "It truly requires wisdom and prudence to tell our own history in pleasing colors to all; yet a brief notice of my morning and noon of life will be of interest to my children and descendants. I was the second child of James and Deziah Griffin, their second son, born in the second month of the year, on the second day of the month, and the second day of the week, and who knows but the second day or week of the moon." These peculiar circumstances attending his birth are both curious and interesting.

I will now make a few remarks on the two great commercial panics of 1837 and 1857, which proved so disastrous to many merchants of this city. I was doing a

large business in provisions during both of
these panics, and was fully prepared to
meet all my engagements without assistance
from any of my friends, or even the banks
where I then kept my accounts. It was in
one of these panics, having plenty of money
on hand, I went to all the banks I knew of
that held my acceptances, and offered to retire them on the spot, they allowing me simple interest at seven per cent. for the time
they had to mature. The banks accepted
my proposition, and I that day paid up all
my acceptances but two which I could not
find. Without any vain-boasting (for that
I despise) I saved several influential firms
from suspending payment by the loan of
money; in fact I was very easy in money
through both of these panics, notwithstanding through one of them I paid five thousand
dollars a day for three months together.

I will now relate two instances of re-
lief I afforded during the last panic. One
of our large lines of canal boats was

in the habit, during the dull season of
freights for this city, of purchasing some
five or six canal boat-loads of corn, to make
freight for their boats, for which they gave
the company's note for thirty days, payable
in New York. This company had five boat-
loads of corn arrive here during the last
panic. They tried in vain to sell their
corn in order to meet their note, then about
falling due; they applied to several of the
large dealers in grain for a loan on it, but
they all had obligations of their own, and
as much as they could stagger under at the
time. At length a deputation of gentlemen
applied to me, representing the difficulty
of this canal line, with a capital of one
million of dollars, and still unable to meet
their note, then maturing, unless they could
raise the amount on the corn. They offered
three per cent. a month for the use of the
money (the then current rate for loans), or
they would pay still more if required. I
finally consented to the arrangement, and

2*

gave them a check for the amount of their note. On the thirty-seventh day after, they sold the corn, and returned me the advance, including the interest of three per cent. a mouth, with their grateful acknowledgments for the favor conferred.

The second case was with a commission merchant in my neighborhood, with whom I was intimately acquainted. He came one evening to my house on Washington Square to see me, as he said, on important business; he finally told me that he would be compelled to stop payment on the morrow unless he could raise a certain amount of money to meet his note or acceptance due the next day. He further stated that he had spent the greater part of that day in calling on his friends for assistance, but without avail; that his store was packed with goods from cellar to garret, but he could find no purchasers who had money. I said to him: "My friend, go home and calm yourself and sleep soundly, and in the morning

call at my office, and I will loan you the
amount you require." His face brightened
and he went home a happy man. A few
days after he returned the loan. That man
has ever been a faithful and sincere friend
to me, for he has never forgotten the kindness I rendered him in his financial trou-
bles.

HUDSON RIVER RAILROAD.

When it was contemplated to build this
road much opposition was manifested in
obtaining subscriptions to the undertaking
by our wealthy men generally, although
it was conceded that it would greatly
advance the interests of this State if it
could be accomplished; but moneyed
men were in doubt whether it would not
be a losing game in the end. At length
Messrs. James Boorman and Thomas Suf-
fern (both wealthy men) put their shoul-
ders to the wheel, and pressed their friends
to lend a helping hand. They applied to

me, and I subscribed for twenty shares, be-
lieving at the same time it would not pay
a dividend for many years to come, but I
was interested to have this road built; for
at that time I was doing a prosperous
commission business in provisions, and I
made up my mind that, if this road could
be finished, I should not be a loser in the
end, if I should never get a dividend on
the stock. The road was at length completed. I never regretted my subscription
to the stock. I derived great advantage
from it. I sold my stock many years ago
at a loss.

CHAPTER V.

TRIP TO NIAGARA.

DURING my residence in Cortlandt Street, some forty-five years ago, I consulted with my wife in relation to our making a trip to Niagara Falls with three of our eldest children. My two eldest sons had just returned home from their boarding-school in the country, to spend their summer vacation; my eldest daughter, also, being at home on her school vacation. It was soon decided to make the tour, and we at once began making preparations for the journey. At that time a trip to Niagara would occupy about the same time that it would now take to visit Europe and return. At the appointed time we started for Albany, having previously made up our minds to travel from Albany by stage and canal alternately, as circumstances might require. At this time there were regular lines of passenger-boats on the canal, and we found the accommodations quite satisfactory. Besides, we found the change from boat to stage, and *vice versa*, very pleasant and refreshing. After arriving at Buffalo, we spent two days in visiting the place and seeing its surroundings—the place was then comparatively small. On our travels from Albany to Buffalo we passed through many interesting scenes along the road. Rochester we found a very desolate-looking place, the streets being full of large and small stumps of trees, which had been removed for the construction of the canal. On other portions of the route we encountered swamps and forests through which the canal had been built. The country in those places looked desolate indeed, but as time has worn on these scenes have been changed from their then desolate-looking wastes into rural culture and beauty.

I beg here to say that my recollections of events that occurred forty-five years ago are much more indistinct to my mind now than those that occurred seventy-five or eighty years ago, for my memory is as fresh now of the scenes and recollections of my youthful days—say from ten years of age—as if they had occurred a month ago, and I believe this fact is generally shared by a great majority of the old men of the present day. With this digression I will proceed with my trip to Niagara.

After leaving Buffalo we reached the Falls in due time. The first view of the cataract, in all the splendor of its magnificence, was, indeed, a sight to fill us with awe and astonishment. Were I capable of giving a description, it would be labor lost, for have they not been described a thousand times by writers and painters of known celebrity? So here I pause. We remained at the Falls two days. On the third day we started for home, stopping on the way to visit Brock's monument, which to me was of little account. Our return was varied, as in going, by stage and canal. If my memory is not at fault we were between three and four weeks in completing the journey. We arrived home in good health and spirits, without accident, well pleased with our trip.

THE INAUGURATION OF GENERAL HARRISON.

At the Inauguration of General Harrison we made up a small party here to proceed to Washington to attend the ceremonies. Mr. N. H. Wolfe, Mr. Philetus Holt, Mr. Sherry of New Bedford, myself, and two or three others (whose names I have forgotten), constituted our party. We left for Washington the previous day and arrived there in the evening. All the hotels were filled to their utmost, and at

first we had some difficulty in securing lodgings, but through the kindness of a friend
we were recommended to a house (a private
boarding-house) kept by a very gentlemanly
Irishman and his wife, where we succeeded
in securing very comfortable quarters.
The cuisine of the establishment, somewhat
to our surprise, compared favorably with
that of many of the prominent hotels.
The landlord and his wife exerted themselves to make us as comfortable as possible. Our supper table was spread with
all the delicacies of the season, and served
to our entire satisfaction. In the morning
after breakfast we repaired to the Capitol,
to witness the Inauguration Ceremonies,
after which we returned to our hotel,
where we found our landlord and wife
had prepared for us a splendid dinner,
which would have done honor to any hotel
in Washington. Iu the evening a few of
our party attended the ball, the others
remaining at home. On the following

morning we left for home, after compli-
menting our landlord and lady on the
elegant manner we had been entertained.
We all arrived in safety, highly pleased
with our trip to Washington.

In connection with the above, I wish to
say that I visited Washington, many years
previous to the visit just spoken of, to
settle some business matters with a resident of that city. This visit occurred
during the administration of General Jackson. While there I concluded to call and
pay my respects to the President. He
received me very graciously, and after a
few remarks I retired.

CHAPTER VII.

THE OLD MAYORS.

I WILL now refer to some of our leading public men and politicians of earlier days. Cadwallader D. Colden was mayor of this city in the earlier part of this century. His residence at the time was on the corner of William and Stone Streets. He was esteemed as a very polished gentleman, and gave frequent entertainments at his house. He was universally beloved by all who knew him. Richard Varick, a gentleman of the old school, was also mayor of this city for a time. His residence at that time was on the corner of Broadway and Pine Street. He was very aristocratic in his general appearance and dress. He invariably wore smallclothes, with silk stockings and silver buckles, in the summer season. He was much esteemed by all who knew him. He was a man of fortune, and passed on through life as a gentleman of leisure.

Walter Bowne, a gentleman of fortune, was another of our early mayors. I can speak of him more definitely, for I was personally acquainted with him, as I have before remarked. I was a tenant six years in one of his houses, and he was, without exception, the best and most accommodating landlord I ever lived under. When I first rented his house he handed me his card with the names of his different mechanics, with directions to call on them for any repairs I might require on the premises, and charge the bills to him. He was one of the most pleasant and agreeable gentlemen I ever knew.

Stephen Allen was mayor of this city for one or two terms. With him and his family I was very early acquainted. He formerly lived in the Bowery, but afterwards removed to the corner of Washington Square and University Place, where he had built, in connection with several of our wealthy citizens, the noble block of buildings fronting the park. I resided twenty-nine years on the block below, running from Fifth Avenue to Macdougal Street. My family, particularly the younger female portion of them, were almost in daily communication with the younger branches of his family, by his second wife, while my own sisters were more intimately associated with his daughters by his first wife. Mr. Allen, for many years, kept a large "duck store;" was successful in business, and at the same time an active politician of the Democratic school, and was for many years one of the sachems of Tammany Hall, with Benjamin Bailey and John Targee, who were the then principal leaders of that day in the Democratic camp. And here permit me to copy, from my favorite poet, Halleck, a few lines from his address to Richard Riker (formerly Recorder of this city for many years), they being so applicable to the three gentlemen above named :

> And Halleck, who has made thy roof,
> Saint Tammany, oblivion proof,
> Thy years illustrious, and thee
> A belted knight of chivalry,
> And changed thy dome of painted bricks,
> And porter casks and politics,
> Into a green Arcadian vale,
> With Stephen Allen for its lark,
> Ben Bailey's voice its watchdog's bark,
> And John Targee its nightingale.

Halleck was a great satirist, as his poem to Fanny will fully testify, for in it he had a hit at all the principal prominent characters of the day. But to return to Mr. Allen. He made a most excellent mayor, and was withal a very honest man. He was self-educated, and a man of strong common sense, with strong prejudices

whenever he took a dislike to any one. He
was kind and good-hearted to all his
friends. Thus much I knew of Stephen
Allen, and now I have a melancholy duty
to perform; that is, the recital of the sad
ending of his life. I was on my way home
from Saratoga, travelling by the Hudson
River Railroad, and when within some
twelve or fifteen miles of the city we discovered a steamer on fire a few miles
ahead of us, which proved to be the Henry
Clay, with her bows turned to the beach,
all in flames from stem to stern. Most of
the passengers who were near the bows
when she struck the beach jumped into the
comparatively shoal water and thus saved
themselves, while others miserably per-
ished. Mr. Allen was found among the
drowned. Our train remained by the scene
for three-quarters of an hour, and brought
many of the rescued to the city. When
the train left the appalling scene Mr.
Allen's body had not been recovered, but

it was found shortly after. Thus ended a busy and useful life.

Philip Hone was mayor of this city for one term, and decidedly one of the most popular mayors this city ever had. Mr. Hone had retired from business some time previous, with an ample fortune. The old firm of John & Philip Hone, auctioneers, were widely known throughout this city for their honesty, industry, and integrity, which gave them unlimited credit, which enabled them to do a large and successful business for many years. Mr. Hone lived during his mayoralty in Broadway, next door to the corner of College Place. It was then esteemed the most beautiful residence in the city. He was mayor when Lafayette arrived here on a visit to this country, and speaking of this great man I would remark, that the enthusiasm throughout the whole country was manifested in a thousand different ways to do honor to him who rendered such important services during our Revolutionary struggle. A magnificent entertainment was given him here at Castle Garden; it took several days to complete the arrangements for this grand fête. Myself, wife, and eldest daughter were present on this occasion. It was a scene always to be remembered, and although fifty years have passed away since then, the scene is as vivid and fresh to my mind now as it was on the night of its celebration. In the morning Lafayette was to leave for Boston. Mayor Hone had prepared at his palatial residence a magnificent breakfast in his honor, to which were invited, with his own private friends, all the officers of the regiment detailed to accompany him from this city. It was a costly and splendid entertainment, and I cannot forbear at the moment again quoting from my old friend Halleck, for the lines are so very appropriate and applicable to Mr. Hone:

3

Oh ! hone a' rie ! oh ! hone a' rie !
   The hymn o'er happy days departed ;
The hope that such again may be,
   When power was large and liberal-hearted,
And wealth was hospitality.

Mr. Andrew H. Mickle was elected mayor after the retirement of Mr. Hone. This election was bought of the sachems of Tammany Hall by Mrs. Russell, the tobacconist and the mother-in-law of the incumbent. She sent a letter to the rulers of Tammany with a pledge to give them $5,000 on condition they would nominate and elect her son-in-law to the office of mayor of this city. The bait was accepted and he was accordingly put in nomination and elected, and the $5,000 promptly paid. He was a man utterly disqualified for the office of mayor, having been brought up behind the tobacco-counter of Mrs. Russell, who then kept in Water near Wall Street. Mrs. Russell was a strong Democrat, and on election days always gave to her work-

men (of whom she employed a large num·
ber) a holiday for electioneering purposes.
Her death was caused by an accident hap·
pening in her own store. As I have said
before, Mr. Mickle was entirely disqualified for the duties of the office, for he was
an uneducated man, and his natural abili-
ties of a very common order, but he was
fortunate in the selection of a young man
of very fair talents (Mr. Ming) to admin-
ister the duties of the office, and matters
proceeded on in a comparatively quiet man·
ner. The father of Mr. Ming was an old
and intimate acquaintance of mine. His
profession was a printer, and for many
years he published the only almanac then
current in this city. He had some peculiarities, one of which was that he never wore
a necktie either in summer or winter—.
his throat was always bare. I have little
or nothing to add to Mr. Mickle's adminis·
tration of the office of mayor, more than
to say that he passed through his duties,

with the aid and assistance of Mr. Ming, quite satisfactorily to the political party which elected him.

Mr. Havemeyer, our late mayor, was elected to the same office some twenty years ago. I knew him personally for many years and, always esteemed him a straightforward and honest man. He was originally a Democrat, and I have reason to believe his bias continued that way.

I now come to my old friend, Mayor Kingsland, of the old firm of D. & A. Kingsland. I have been personally acquainted with this gentleman for many years, and frequently visited his house on Fifth Avenue, where he still resides. I had been in the habit, for years, of supplying their vessels with provisions until they abandoned that branch of their business. Mr. Kingsland, when mayor, gave general satisfaction in his administration of the office, and was universally esteemed as an honest public servant.

With the politicians of the present day I never intermeddle, but I always vote at every election. I have always been a Whig and Republican. I never sought for office, for the simple reason I never wanted one. The life of a professional politician is, at the best, a roving one, and subject to many changes in the political turn of the wheel. Of the later incumbents of the mayor's office I know but little, and the present generation of politicians are much better posted in regard to their merits and demerits than I am. Therefore I have no more to say on this subject.

The most celebrated surgeons and physicians of the olden time, some fifty or sixty years ago, were Hosack, Post, Stevens, Mott, and Cheesman, and many others whose names I do not recollect. In divinity we had Dr. Wainwright, Dr. Potts, Dr. Mason, who stood at the head of the profession, Dr. Milledoler, Dr. Livingston, Dr. Hobart, Dr. Spring, Dr. Hawks, Dr. Adams, and several others of equal celebrity. Dr. Adams is the only one now living; the remainder have all gone to reap their reward. At this present time we have many clergymen of equal power and ability, who compare most favorably with their predecessors.

In looking back, some seventy or eighty years, my mind becomes confused in bringing to my memory a thousand little incidents that have occurred in this city, which might prove somewhat interesting to the present generation if I had the memory and skill to relate them. But if any of them should flash on my mind during the recital of this short history, I will add them to these pages before they are closed.

And here I have a word or two to say on my own account. It strikes me very forcibly that the inflation of the currency, which bill has been so long the leading topic of discussion in Congress, and which has been passed by both houses in direct opposition to all our leading mercantile men of the country, is a strong evidence to me that one-half its members are totally unfit for the stations they occupy. We want experienced merchants and bankers in place of lawyers and professional politicians to legislate on financial subjects, so vital to the credit, and honor, and future welfare of our country. We unfortunately have in our legislative halls many unprincipled men, who only desire to carry out their own views.

April 24, 1874.—My evening paper, "The Commercial Advertiser," of yesterday gave me the pleasing and gratifying intelligence of the veto of the Expansion Currency Bill. I rejoice that President Grant had the firmness and conviction of his duty to himself as well as to the citizens generally, to crush out a bill so evidently injurious to the credit and honor of our country, as well as to a great majority of our fellow-citizens; for, in the event of its having been sustained, it might have enriched a few and caused ruin to many. These are my views on this subject, and may be taken for what they are worth, but if I mistake not the majority will coincide with my opinion.

CHAPTER VII.

LITERARY, ETC.

THERE are so many circumstances, and such a variety of incidents that have occurred during my morning, noon, and decline in life, that my memory fails me, and I am unable to grasp many important events that should be contained in this history, as well as many events of minor importance that would not particularly interest my friends or readers. Hence when a flash of some important incident crosses my mind I at once note it down, however inapplicable it may be to my previous observations. There are many brilliant and beautiful writers in the present day, but, as I have before remarked, the names of Irving and Cooper will live when

3*

the great mass of the present writers will be forgotten.

I wish again to pay a slight tribute to one of my favorites, Mr. John G. Saxe. I have always admired this man; his poetry has an expression that will convey to the most uncultivated mind the ideas he portrays.

The literary productions of years ago, compared with the present time, were very meagre. I am of course only alluding to our own country. There have sprung into existence so many that gain a livelihood by writing that their name is legion. Some good, many worthless. But in looking back and remembering, as I well do, the beautiful stories of Irving and Cooper, and making comparison with the writers of the present day, I fail to find their equals, and I fear it will yet be long before they are matched. I read and have read to me so much, that I feel competent to judge of this question without any egotism on my part.

When I first thought of writing these papers, I proclaimed that, in the event of my doing so, I would not have them published until after my death; but after having commenced them, several of my friends insisted on having them published during my lifetime. After reflecting on the subject, I finally made up my mind to do so, in case I completed them before that event took place. In contemplating my own dissolution at no distant day, I feel perfectly reconciled to the will of my Heavenly Father. He has already prolonged my life far beyond the ordinary age of man. He has blest me in giving me liberally of the good things of this world, but in my later years He has seen fit to withdraw from me the greater portion of that independence I once possessed.

There are such an infinitude of subjects connected with the history of a long, active business life, that it requires much time and thought to get at the more salient points of interest, and communicate the same in pleasing and glowing colors to your friends; there are such a great variety of subjects treated on at the present day by writers of known ability and influence, many of them professional writers, that I am almost constrained at times to lay aside my pen and consign to the waste-basket what little I have written, as of little or no use to my fellow-beings. But if happily there should be a few passages worth preserving by my friends, I shall be satisfied. There are various systematic writers who acquire for themselves and families a fine support, and many of them become independent.

CHAPTER VIII.

MY BIRTHDAY.

MAY 29, 1874.—This is my eighty-ninth birthday. I now enter on my ninetieth year. When I look back on my past life it simply appears as a dream. I have lived nineteen years longer than the time allotted to man, through the interposition of a Divine Providence, but for what cause or end I know not. Were a man to live a thousand years it would be but a very short period of time when compared with the eternity that follows. Eternity! that dreadful thought of untried beings. Some fifty years ago I heard a sermon preached by the Rev. Hooper Cumming, son of General Cumming, then of Newark, New Jersey, in which he said: "With the dead

time ceases to be, till the resurrection of
the body, whether that event occurs in a
thousand or tens of thousands of years;
hence its identity and freshness will be like
a morning dream." Before Adam was created by the fiat of Almighty God millions
of ages had rolled on, and will continue to
roll on through the ceaseless ages of eternity.   Philosophers tell us there are
planets so remote in space that there has
not been time for their light to reach our
globe since its creation. The thoughts of
man cannot grasp the boundless creations
of Almighty God, and not until the resurrection of our mortal bodies into spiritual
existence, may we begin to learn the
heights and depths of the wonder-working
powers of the Godhead.

There has been for many years a fixed
principle of belief in my mind (although I
have not met with the idea in any writings
that have come under my observation),
that every intelligent being born into this

world has born within him a little world
of his own, which is as distinct from that of
any other being as the features of one face
differ from another. There is a mystery
in- relation to this within us—that we
cannot communicate to our best and dearest
friends the subtle influences that govern
this inner life, however liberally endowed
with talents of the most brilliant order;
there is no language in which we can begin
to convey, or even describe, the workings
of this little world within us. It may be
called by many one of the thousand Isms
that abound with our theologians, but for
myself I know it to be a truth with me
as sure as I know I am a live and moral
being.

I must avail myself once more of a
quotation from my favorite poet Halleck;
it so fully illustrates my present age and
condition; with the exception of the last
six lines, which I cannot appropriate to
myself, but which are necessary to fill out

the beautiful poetic inspiration of the
author:

> But many are my years, and few
> Are left me ere night's holy dews
> And sorrow's holier tears will keep
> The grass green, when in Death I sleep.
> And when that grass is green above me,
> And those that *bless me now, and love me,*
> Are sleeping by my side,
> Will it avail me aught that men
> Tell to the world with lip and pen
> That once I lived and died?
> No! If a garland for my brow
> Is growing, let me have it now,
> While I'm alive to wear it;
> And if in whispering my name
> There's music in the voice of fame,
> Like Garcia's, let me hear it.

As previously observed, the last six lines
I disclaim all appropriation of to myself,
for the reason I never had the vanity to
believe that any public or private act of
mine ever entitled me to a "garland for
my brow," or to any fame beyond what

any of my fellow-citizens are entitled, who pass through life with the reputation of honest industry and integrity of character.

CHAPTER IX.

THE OLD CITY HOTEL.

This old building was demolished many years ago.   In 1800 it was one of the most prominent landmarks in the lower part of this city, and it appeared almost a sacrilege to blot it out of existence.*   When I recur back to the many happy hours I have spent under its roof, and bring to my memory those (all dead and gone) who were my contemporaries, it makes me sad indeed.

---

* There are many interesting associations connected with the old City Hotel, that will remain with me through life. During my residence in Cortlandt Street I was a frequent visitor there.   Mr. Charruaud, so well known to all old New Yorkers, had his dancing-school there, and those of my children who were old enough, attended it.   It became a general rendezvous for the meeting of friends on their return from business to their homes.

It was in this hotel that our musical entertainments were given. In this hotel assembled the beauty and fashion of the
city, but it has vanished from the scene.
But what a history it might tell of lives
made miserable, and of those made happy!
In recording these recollections of the old
landmarks of this city, and remembering,
as I well do, the social hours passed among
them, it is a pleasure to look back, and
again, in imagination, visit the scenes of so
much pleasure and enjoyment.

THE ASTOR HOUSE.

This house has become one of the old
landmarks of our city, and its proprietors,
the Messrs. Stetson, deserve the praise of
all. It has been conducted in such a way
that it has drawn within its portals the
greatest statesmen of the country. It has
for many years been the rendezvous of the
chiefs of the Republican party. The Hon.

Daniel Webster had his rooms at this house whenever he visited the city. I have but few associations connected with this hotel beyond those Republican leaders. In fact, the Astor House has always been considered one of the best conducted hotels in this country.

THE NEW YORK HOTEL.

This hotel was built many years ago. It occupies one entire block. There was formerly on this ground a large double frame building occupied for many years as a public-house. I distinctly recollect, some forty or ·more years ago, of being invited by a number of acquaintances to join them in patronizing a once prominent broker, who became unfortunate, and who was at that time the proprietor of the above-named premises. I joined the party, consisting of some thirty ·or forty, and proceeded on a Saturday afternoon to a dinner

of green turtle at one dollar a head. At
that time we had no public stages, so we
concluded to walk there and back instead
of hiring coaches for this purpose. Suffice
it to say we had a very pleasant entertainment, and returned home in good condition
by bedtime. During the Yellow Fever
Year those of us who were members of the
Exchange arranged with the landlord of
this house to meet there daily from twelve
to two o'clock, and thus we held our regular meetings until the abatement of the
fever and our return down-town.

There are many pleasing associations connected with the New York Hotel. Living
for so many years adjacent to it, I was
in the habit of visiting there very often,
and being intimate with the landlords I
was almost as much at home as at my
own house. The associations and new acquaintances formed there have left a
pleasing recollection on my mind that I
can never forget. At that time I was very

fond of the game of billiards, and often joined in the amusement. Although I was far from being a skilful player, there were, however, many others no better than myself, and hence I as often won as lost a game. For many years past there has been wonderful improvement in this scientific game, and the skill exercised in the great matches, now often played, draw together hundreds of persons to witness them. But it is now a number of years since my failing eyesight has prevented me from witnessing any of these great matches, were I disposed so to do. My friend, Colonel Isaac H. Reed, an old boarder at this hotel, was very fond of this game; he was a bold, dashing player—he understood the game perfectly.

Previous to our civil war this hotel was the favorite resort of most of our Southern visitors; it still continues to receive their patronage. Since its erection it has had several landlords, but I have always understood that they were well patronized and retired with ample means. May success attend the present occupants !

WASHINGTON HALL.

This building was erected some fifty or sixty years ago, on the site of Stewart's wholesale dry-goods store, by the then political party called Federalists, of which Isaac Seabring was president at that time. It was a large hotel, and kept by a Captain Croker for many years. At the close of our war of 1812 there was a splendid banquet given in honor of the occasion in this hotel by the aristocracy of our city, in which the renowned Dominick Lynch presided. I was told by two or three of my personal friends who were present on that occasion, that it was certainly the most spendid and brilliant display of beauty and fashion that had ever before been seen in this city. The great majority of the participants are now in their graves.

Louis Napoleon during his visit to this country made this hotel his headquarters. There is one fact well authenticated—that for several years previous to its demolition there was a large club of our most influential merchants who met there nightly for the express purpose of gambling; and more than a dozen names (now in their graves) I am familiar with to this day, but both honor and delicacy forbid my using them. Unfortunately one respectable blackleg got an introduction to this club, and was elected a member; soon after he displayed his cloven foot by secreting in his coatsleeve some important cards, and was at length detected in using one of them to great advantage. This created a great row, and he was expelled from the club on the spot; by some means the news got out the next day, and created much excitement at the time.

The Federalists, who erected Washington Hall, did not flourish many years, and eventually disbanded altogether. Their members finally united themselves with the Democratic or Whig organizations.

There was a book published here many years ago called "The Federalist." The articles it contained were contributed by the ablest writers of the day, and had an extensive circulation. There may be copies of the work still on hand in some of the leading bookstores, or they may be extinct. Washington Hall was finally purchased by Mr. Stewart, and on its site is erected the stately store, sacred to dry-goods and Mr. Stewart.

CHAPTER X.

THE CHOLERA OF 1832.

THERE are many thrilling incidents that have occurred in this city within the past forty or fifty years. The cholera, which broke out here in 1832, raged fearfully, and a large proportion of the citizens left the city for different parts of the country. I then resided with my family in Cortlandt Street, and, singular as it may appear, every family in this street, but my own and one other, between Broadway and Greenwich Street, left the city. I remained with my family throughout the epidemic. My store at this time was in Broad Street, near Front. I had a colored servant living with me at this time. He and myself were the only two persons who left the door of my house for six weeks. We adopted regular rules of government in my family, under the advice of my family physician, Dr. Stephen Brown. I always had in my house the usual remedies then in use. I went regularly to Washington Market every morning after breakfast. I bought the best fresh beef and steaks for one day, and young chickens to roast or broil the next. On my return from market I went to my store, and there was scarcely a morning, for two months, that I did not meet on Broadway from three to six ambulances, with cholera patients on their way to the hospital in the Park, formerly the old jail, but now the Hall of Records. I became so familiar with these scenes daily in going to my office and returning home, that they did not seem to affect my usual nervous temperament. I left my store at four o'clock, and remained home until the next morning. My family escaped this epi-

demic, with one exception. One of my
daughters, twelve or thirteen years of age,
was suddenly taken with all the symptoms.
We administered at once the remedies pre-
scribed, and dispatched my servant with
all haste for our physician, who fortunately was at home, and they returned together. The doctor was with her for six
hours, when he pronounced her in safety
and left for home. In many cases the patients died in six hours from the first
attack. It was very malignant and fatal.

Some few years earlier we were visited
with the yellow fever, which spread death
and destruction throughout the city. A
large proportion of the inhabitants removed from the city. My family then resided in Frankfort Street, near Pearl and
Franklin Square. I removed my family
to New Windsor, Orange County, closing
my house, with hundreds of other families.
Several of my friends and neighbors removed above Spring Street, on the North

River, erected shanties, and removed a portion of their goods from their stores down town, and continued their business; for at that time a greater portion of the property between Spring Street and the old State Prison was vacant lots, and that portion of the city was entirely free from the fever, being nearly two miles distant from the infected district. A fence had also been erected across the city from the North to the East River, somewhere above Canal Street, and it was considered dangerous to go below those limits. I procured room for a desk in Mr. Charles Dennison's shanty, which he had erected for the purpose of his grocery business, and several merchants procured board and lodging with a Mr. John Montaigne, who kept a small house in Greenwich Street. I boarded with him, but slept nightly on board one of the Newburg or New Windsor packets (which lay in the immediate neighborhood), for I was intimately acquainted with all the captains. On every Saturday I left the city to visit my family, and returned on Monday morning. If my memory serves me, I think they were absent about two months, and glad indeed was I to have them once more around me.

Soon after this I removed with my family to Cortlandt Street, paying a rental of $700 a year for the house I occupied. I had a lease of this house for six years. At the expiration of this lease I removed to the house of Philip Hone, Esq., a few doors below, at a rental of $1,000 a year. This house was built by Mr. Hone for his own residence, where he resided for a number of years. I had a lease of this house for five years. I remained in it but four years, having bought a house on Washington Square, but I had no difficulty in covering the last year of my lease at the same rental. So on the 1st of May, 1837, I removed to my new house on Washington Square, where I resided twenty-nine years

—twenty-five years in great prosperity, after which my fortunes began to wane.

As I have already related in other portions of these sketches many pleasing incidents of my life, I am not now inclined to dwell on the sad and shady side of my later days; but I must here remark, that I have believed for many years that great wealth does not constitute great happiness. There are many other qualities in man's nature that contribute more pleasure and happiness than mere riches, however much their possessor may prize them. I have been in affluence; but the natural cheerfulness of my nature, with my usually good health, renders my declining years peaceful and quiet, with very moderate means.

I am now living with my daughter at the Washington Hotel, No. 1 Broadway. We have very comfortable quarters on the first floor, overlooking the Battery. We have our private table served to us in my parlor. The table is excellent in every respect, but as for myself I have been in the habit for the past thirty years of taking but two meals a day—my breakfast at eight to half-past eight and my dinner at six o'clock; and I consider that this mode of living, with my well-known temperance habits, has been largely conducive to my present length of years.

This day, April 6, 1874, I am eighty eight years, ten months and nine days old, and in excellent health. I spend from two to two and a half hours each day on our Produce Exchange, of which I am an honorary member. My present business is very limited, but I have a few old customers who invariably come or send to me to supply their vessels with beef and pork for stores. I have been in active business so long (sixty-five years) that I should be very unhappy if I could not get on 'Change daily, and meet my old friends and acquaintances. I have been so long a time in harness that I love it, and it fits me so well I am determined to live and die in it. I have always taken great pleasure in doing business, and allow me here to remark, for it is well known that many merchants, when the day is over, carry to their homes the cares and anxieties relating to their business; and these cares so often afflict and distress them, that they do not enjoy the pleasant associations and intercourse with their families with which they are pleasantly surrounded, but it has not been so with me. When the day was over I returned home free from these anxieties, and enjoyed myself in the companionship of my family.

There is one suggestion which I wish to impress upon the rising young merchants of this city. I have observed in many instances merchants retiring from business in middle life, after procuring a sufficiency to satisfy them, and I have noticed that after a year or two they usually become discontented and unhappy, anxiously wish-

4*

ing themselves back again to their old
haunts of business. Many of them die
within six or eight years after their retirement, while some, after seeking happiness
for two or three years (which they cannot
find), again return to their old occupations,
either as active or special partners. My
recommendation to young merchants, when
once established in a good and thriving
business, is to hold to it as long as their
health and mental capacity qualify them
for it; and I am bold to say that this course
will not only add to their length of days,
but to their happiness through life.

Many years ago, while doing a prosper
ous business, I was asked by several of my
acquaintances why I did not retire. My
reply was: "If I knew for a certainty that
by continuing in business I should actually
lose $5,000 a year during my life, I should
continue as long as I had the $5,000 a
year to lose, for nothing would render me
more unhappy than to have nothing to

employ my mind." It must not be supposed, however, that during my long business life I had no relaxation from business. For thirty years of my life my
family and myself were in the habit of
visiting the Springs and other watering-
places. Among our favorite resorts were
Saratoga, West Point, and Newport.
These were the three principal watering
resorts thirty years ago. For twenty-five
years in succession I visited Saratoga
Springs (with one exception). My family
usually remained at one of these places
during most of the summer. The United
States Hotel at Saratoga was my favorite
resort. We generally ended the summer
at Cozzens' Hotel, West Point. It was my
custom to return home once a week while
my family remained at either of the afore-
said places, returning to them in the course
of two or three days. These excursions I
enjoyed very much, and when we all
finally returned home from our summer

pleasures and amusements, it gave a new zest and pleasure to our own home comforts and enjoyments.

TRIP TO PATERSON.

On the 4th of July, 1832, Mr. Charles Denison, Henry Wykoff, Benjamin Stagg and myself (by invitation of Mr. Denison) visited Paterson to pass the day in social enjoyment. After visiting the different factories and partaking of a substantial meal, we returned. On our way to the city we heard there had been several cases of cholera reported. We hesitated to rely upon these reports, but it was soon an established fact. I have alluded in these pages to the dreadful havoc existing during the prevalence of this fearful scourge.

The three gentlemen above-named were associated so intimately with me, that, when I recur back and think of the pleasant reminiscences connected in our intercourse with each other, I can remember nothing

but pleasure. But still in looking back
and knowing, as I well do, that I am almost
alone on the scene, melancholy reflections
will arise. In paying this small tribute to
my departed friends a few lines have occurred to me, which I quote:

> Eternal Hope, when yonder spheres sublime
> Pealed their first notes to sound the march of time,
> Thy joyous youth began, but not to fade.
> When all the sister-planets have decayed,
> When, wrapped in flames, the realms of ether glow
> And heaven's last thunder shakes the world below,
> Thou undismayed shalt o'er the ruins smile,
> And light thy torch at Nature's funeral pile.

This quotation is from Campbell's Pleasures of Hope, and is completely entwined
around my very being. I repeat these
lines with many favorite ones almost nightly on my retiring to bed. They calm the
tumults that often oppress me.

CHAPTER XI.

MILITARY.

I PURPOSE now to make a few remarks upon a few of my old military friends. I was intimately acquainted with Major-General Scott for many years. He became very distinguished with his countrymen, and very justly so. I distinctly recollect when he first came to this city, and was stationed at the old Fort now called Castle Garden on the Battery. It was at West Point where I became more intimately acquainted with him, for I had been in the habit, for many years, of spending several weeks there with my family during the summer, and the General, during that season, always made this place his headquarters. I always found him a very agreeable companion. He was extravagantly fond of playing whist, and would frequently send for me to make up the match when one or two were wanted to complete it. I was, comparatively speaking, a poor player in comparison with many others then, who were highly skilful in the game in which the General stood prominent. He always preferred playing dummy, and would always give two points to his opponents when so playing. I shall never forget the observation he once made while he and myself were partners in a game in which we were beaten. Nothing vexed him more than to be beaten at cards or chess. His remark was, that " Mr. Hubbard is the poorest player I ever met with." I was by no means a good player, as I did not take sufficient interest in it to keep my mind accurately informed of the cards previously played, hence I was frequently at fault in my play. The General was also a skilful chess-player, of which game I was totally ignorant. We occasionally played billiards together, and although I was not a skilful player, I could beat the General very easily, but he never took much interest in billiards; chess and whist were his favorite amusements. The General was a universal favorite with all who knew him; he was very companionable and easy in his manners and address, and the cadets almost worshipped him. He was well deserving the grateful homage of his countrymen; he has passed away—peace to his ashes.

When I was a young man, twenty-five or thirty years of age, I was well acquainted with General Stevens; he was an old Knickerbocker, sixty or seventy years ago. His residence was in Beekman Street, and his store in South Street, between Beekman and Peck Slip. He had a large family of sons, but no daughters. One of his sons was president of the Bank of Commerce for many years, which he conducted with ability and success, and from which

he retired, a few years since, from the infirmities of old age. Another of General
Stevens' sons was a celebrated surgeon and
physician. General Stevens was a large
importer of French brandies and other
merchandise. He has been dead for many
years.

General Morton was Commander-in-Chief
for many years of the military of this city,
and also for many years secretary of the
Board of Aldermen through all its political changes. He was always nominated
by every new board without regard to
politics. In fact, he had become so familiar with the duties of the office, that each
new board applied to him for information
on various matters which they knew he
perfectly understood. The General was
highly respected by all classes of his fellow-citizens.

General Hopkins, of the old firm of
Hopkins & Hawley, was a fellow-soldier
with me in the regiment and company I

joined in 1809. Our company was composed of the best class of young men in the city, and we took rank as and were pronounced the best drilled company in the regiment. Our drill-room was at Williams' Hotel in the Bowery, a short distance above Chatham Street. One evening we had an election for sergeant. I was nominated for the office, which I very promptly declined, and I forthwith nominated Mr. Hopkins, and he was elected. Mr. Hopkins was a younger member than I by a few months only, and at the end of my seven years service Mr. Hopkins was Lieutenant-Colonel of the Regiment, and was afterwards appointed General of the Division. Our company usually gave one ball during the winter, and I was invariably appointed one of the managers as well as one of the supper-committee. These entertainments were very pleasant and agreeable, and many lasting friendships grew out of these yearly reunions. Gen-

eral Hopkins died several years ago, both
honored and respected by all who knew
him.

. General Hall, who died the latter part
of May last, I had been very intimately
acquainted with during the past fifty years.
He formerly kept his music store opposite
Franklin Square, at the intersection of
Pearl and Cherry Streets; from thence he
removed to Broadway many years ago. I
first became more particularly acquainted
with him during the existence of the old
Sacred Musical Society of this city, in
which he took a great and lively interest.
It was the General who was the cause of
my election to the presidency of that society, without my knowledge or consent. I
have before alluded to this fact. The
General took great pride in his military
duties. He was a mild, quiet, and amiable
gentleman. I frequently patronized his
music store during my musical mania,
which absorbed most of my leisure hours

for many years. But my age as well as
my sight and hearing prevent me from
participating any longer in the pleasure of
the Opera, and hence I must content myself with the retrospect of the pleasures I
once enjoyed, and live them over again in
imagination.   And here I honestly admit I
derive much pleasure from this indulgence.

CHAPTER XII.

THE OPERA AND MUSICAL CELEBRITIES OF THE PAST.

It is said every man has his hobby. I was always passionately fond of music. Thirty years ago I was a member of every musical society in this city. I was elected one year, without my knowledge or consent, president of the Sacred Musical Society. I was absent from the meeting at the time of the election, never having aspired to any official office, social or political. I tendered, at the next meeting, my resignation, which they declined to accept, therefore I served the society for one year to the best of my ability. Philip Hone and Dr. Rockwell were previous presidents. This society numbered about three hundred active members.

During the year I was president we gave four concerts. At one of these we had engaged Mr. and Mrs. Wood (of English fame), and also Mr. Montressor, of the Italian Opera, a splendid tenor. The house was packed from dome to pit. Mr. Wood was the first to appear. He sang a favorite song, and was much applauded. The next on the programme was the Italian tenor. He sang his solo magnificently, and at the close the whole house thundered forth their applause in repeated shouts of praise. Mrs. Wood was next on the programme, and the time of her appearance having been delayed (from some cause unknown to the audience, or even to myself who presided), I was sent for to come to her room under the stage, the messenger telling me she was in great distress. I hurried down and found her in tears, and apparently suffering. I asked, "Are you

ill? If so I will call in a physician, for
there are a half dozen or more in the
house." She said, "No, no; I will be better soon." I then entreated her to tell me
the cause of her apparent suffering, and she
finally told me the cause of her distress.
It was that the Italian tenor had received all
the applause, and her husband but very little. I laughed and soon talked her into good
humor; the audience in the meantime were
clamorous and noisy, having waited at least
fifteen minutes for her appearance. I at
length led her up to the platform, and she
was received with shouts of applause.

Mrs. Wood had at this time no equal or
rival on the English or American stage.
On this occasion she sang with more energy
and spirit than I had ever heard her. She
absolutely appeared inspired, and communicated that inspiration to the audience.
I never witnessed a greater outburst of applause. Cheer followed cheer, the audience rising, and it was "encore, encore,"

from two thousand voices. At length
order was restored, and she again repeated
her song with marvellous effect. The
audience would not then be satisfied, but
kept up the applause till she came again
to the front and gave them a new song before the audience would release her. During the remainder of the evening I never saw
a being more perfectly happy and joyful.

It was on the advent of Malibran and
Sontag that the popularity of Mrs. Wood
began to wane. It was related to me by
Mr. Charles E. Horn (an English tenor
and pianist, who resided in this city many
years, and sung in English Opera at the old
Park Theatre for several years), that on
Malibran's first appearance on the English
stage he had taken an early seat in the pit
of Covent Garden Theatre. A rôle in the
opera had been assigned her, against which
she vehemently protested with the manager, but in vain. "You," she said, "are
master to-night, but in the future I shall

be your master and choose my own rôles."
The fact was, Mrs. Wood took the first
rôle and Malibran was assigned the second.
"The house," said Horn, "was packed
from dome to pit. On singing her aria
she absolutely electrified the audience, and
they all arose with shouts of delight. She
repeated her aria, but at its close the
storm of applause was as great as ever.
She came forward and sang an aria from
another opera, with the same results. She
then ordered a piano that stood at the
back of the stage, and sang an English
song to her own accompaniment. She
then retired behind the scenes, and was
careful in doing so to pass the manager,
who had been listening to her throughout
this wonderful scene. As she passed him,
he lifted his hat and said, ' You have con-
quered and you are my master now.' During this wonderful performance of Malibran Mrs. Wood was in her dressing-room,
crying like a child."

5

When the Garcia company first arrived in this country they came under the engagement and auspices of Dominick Lynch, Esq., who, while visiting Europe, came in contact with this troupe. Mr. Lynch was considered one of our most fashionable citizens. He engaged the company, consisting of Mr. and Mrs. Garcia, son and daughter, for the Park Theatre, then under the management of Mr. Simpson. Their first appearance was in the opera of the "Barber of Seville." They came here unheralded by fame, but with the influence of Mr. Lynch all the lower tier of boxes were taken by our then fashionable and aristocratic citizens. The opera was a great success. The daughter was quite young, being but seventeen years of age. The Barber was sung three times with increased enthusiasm, after which several other operas were placed upon the stage. They continued to increase in popularity. Old Garcia was a splendid tenor, but he was a

great tyrant, and compelled his daughter
to study eight hours each day. It was
during her engagement here that a Mr.
Malibran fell desperately in love with her,
and offered her father $20,000 if he would
consent to allow his daughter to become
his wife. Mr. Malibran was a merchant in
South Street. The bargain was finally
consummated; she, it was said, to release
herself from the tyranny of her father, for
Malibran was old enough to be her father.
Within sixty days after their marriage
Malibran failed in business, and she soon
after cut loose from him; and on her own
responsibility made an engagement with
the manager of the Bowery Theatre to sing
there. I attended all her performances in
this city.

Shortly after the close of her engagement at the Bowery Theatre she left for
Europe, under the protection of Peter Harmony, Esq., and Malibran soon after followed her to France, but she would have

nothing to do or say to him. She soon obtained a divorce from him, and shortly after married De Beriot, at this time one of the most celebrated violinists in France. She soon after made an engagement to sing at the Italian Opera in Paris, where she won fresh laurels. Her fame soon reached St. Petersburg, and an agent was dispatched from that capital to Paris to secure an engagement from her to sing in that city. She accepted the very liberal offers made her, and soon she and her husband started by stage-coach for their destination. There were no railroads then. In many parts of the country through which they passed her fame had preceded her, and had reached many of the inhabitants along the route they were travelling; and at one hotel where it was known the stage would stop for change of horses and refreshments, the country people for some twenty miles around assembled, determined to hear her sing. When they

arrived at the hotel they found it surrounded by a small army of people, and
when it was made known to her that the
gathering had assembled to hear her sing,
she kindly said to the landlord to an-
nounce to the people assembled that as
soon as she rested from the fatigue of her
journey, she would willingly comply with
their request. In a short time De Beriot,
with his wife and his violin, advanced to
the verandah that surrounded the hotel, and
she sang three or four songs, which perfectly astonished them with wonder and
delight. Her hearers then made up a
purse of gold of $100, and deputed one of
their number to present it to her; but she
politely refused it, saying she had been
as much pleased and delighted in convey-
ing pleasure to them as they had been in
listening to her songs.

Shortly after they resumed their journey, arriving at length at St. Petersburg.
Soon after their arrival they were called

upon by the Chamberlain of the Emperor,
who communicated to them the usages and
the etiquette of the court in relation to the
Opera. In the first place she was directed
to write a polite note to the Emperor and
his family, requesting them to graciously
attend the opera on her first performance.
She was also further told that the custom
was that no prima donna was permitted to
be applauded in the presence of the royal
family until she was first heard to sing.
This last prohibition she at once protested
against, and she directed a note to the
Emperor and his family not to attend her
first performance at the opera, in consequence of her not being permitted to be applauded on her first entrance on the stage,
for with that prohibition she could not
sing at all. The Emperor read her note,
and was so much pleased with it that he
forthwith directed his Chamberlain to call
on Malibran and inform her that he and
his family would honor the opera on her

first appearance, and would see to it that she got the applause she required on her first entrance upon the stage. It was a perfect triumph; her fame resounded throughout the empire, and agents came from every quarter to secure her at the close of her engagement at St. Petersburg. She received from the royal family many valuable presents, and from the nobility gifts without number. She was the idol of their idolatry, and had free access to the palace. Her whole soul was full, for she lived and breathed in the applause of the world. She had no rivals, and was happy.

She died young in London, where she had gone to attend a celebrated musical festival many years ago. The writer has heard all the celebrated musical celebrities that have visited this city from Europe, but he has never heard but one Malibran. Peace to her ashes. My next great favorite was Alboni, the most splendid con-

tralto of this or any former age, as far as
we have any account. She came to New
York about the same time that the celebrated Sontag arrived here, who was indeed a splendid actress as well as singer;
but she had seen her best days, while Alboni was in the zenith of her wonderful
powers. I have not language to describe
her. She sang without any apparent ef-
fort, and a flood of surpassing melody
flowed forth like the joyous singing of the
nightingale. I was early introduced to her,
and we became very intimate friends. Her
husband, who was a Count, was a very
pleasant and agreeable person. They had
rooms at the New York Hotel, and as my
family resided on Washington Square I
called at their rooms quite frequently, and
she would always sit at the piano and sing
for me when I requested the favor of her.
She and her husband visited Saratoga
Springs during the summer, and several
members of my own family spent several

weeks there. During their stay at Saratoga she gave several concerts, to the delight and gratification of its numerous visitors. After their return to this city she gave three or four concerts at Tripler Hall in Broadway. I never missed hearing her sing while in this city. At her last concert, previous to her leaving for her home in Paris, I called on her, during the interval of the concert, to say good-bye. She gave me a most pressing invitation to visit her at her home in Paris, if I ever came there. She still remains (I am told) at the head of her profession. Several of our Americans who had seen her in Paris told me she invariably inquired of them if I was still living and well.

A number of years previous to Alboni's visit to this country another celebrated singer arrived here—Caradori Allan—well known and highly respected by our old Knickerbockers. She gave her concerts at the old City Hotel. I was shortly after

introduced to her and to her husband; they
then boarded in Murray Street. I became
very much attached to her, for she was not
only a perfect lady but a most superb
vocalist, and I never missed one of her
concerts. During her stay here she was
prevailed upon by her husband to accept
a short engagement to sing at the Park
Theatre. Her husband was a Scotchman by
birth, and very much of a gentleman, and
very fond of money, it was said. She was
no actress, but made up for that defect in
the beauty and splendor of her voice. I engaged five seats in the boxes for her whole
engageemnt, which proved a great success,
both to her and the manager, Mr. Simpson.
I gave a musical entertainment at my house
on Washington Square in her honor. During the evening she sang three or four of
her English songs. A few days after they
left for their home in England, and the
day previous to their departure they called
at my house and left their farewell cards.

These musical recollections have afforded me much pleasure in the retrospect, for there has scarcely been a day, during the past sixty years, that I have not thought and reflected on the pleasure they gave me. In regard to my own family I had but one real musical child. I discovered at an early age, while she was taking lessons of Mr. Charles E. Horn on the piano, that she had a very sweet musical voice. One afternoon on entering my house, on my return from my office, I heard from my parlor a voice singing a simple melody that I had never heard before. I was enchanted with the voice, and remained listening in the hall until it ceased. I then rushed into the parlor, placed my arms about my daughter's neck and kissed her, expressing the great pleasure and delight at her beautiful voice, for I had never before heard her sing. She was then twelve years old, and, as before stated, she was taking piano lessons of Mr. Horn, who was a most accomplished singer, and he had that day given her a simple little ballad, having discovered she had a very beautiful voice. It was after her teacher had gone that she was rehearsing the lesson he had given her. The next time I saw Mr. Horn he complimented me on the beautiful voice of his pupil. From that time forward, until her nineteenth year, I employed the best musical talent to instruct her, that could be obtained in this city.

Rapetti, the celebrated violinist and conductor of the Italian Opera in this city, gave her two or three lessons a week for three years, until he met me one day and said, "I have instructed your daughter until I am unable to teach her any more than she knows herself, and I honestly tell you that it is only throwing away the money you pay me to continue me any longer in your employ." She had acquired under his teaching a very perfect knowledge of the Italian language, which she preferred in singing to the English. Her voice was a mezzo-soprano of superior quality, and one of the most sympathetic I ever heard. They called her a Malibran.

For two winters I gave musical entertainments at my house on Washington Square, once every fortnight, to which cards were sent out for the course to my musical friends, and I undertake to say they were the most celebrated ever given in this city twenty-seven or twenty-eight years ago. All the best musical talent attended. Solos, duets, trios, quartets, and choruses were performed with great perfection; in addition, two glee clubs were usually in attendance. I instituted these entertainments for the more particular purpose of accustoming my daughter to sing before large and appreciating audiences.

I cannot forbear mentioning an incident that occurred one evening at the close of one of these entertainments. A deputation of six musical gentlemen waited upon me and said, "It is a great pity and almost a sin that the lovers of music generally could not hear your daughter sing. Now, if you and your daughter will consent to five public concerts, we will engage to pay her $500 a night for five songs or duets each night." I replied, "I had not educated my daughter for the stage, and further I was then in a position that neither of us were necessitated to accept the pecuniary offer." She sang for me almost every evening when at home, and when our windows were open in summer, there would gather in the park and street in front of my house hundreds of people to listen and enjoy her magic voice.

In the month of June, while the Astor Place Opera-house was still open, Badialli, the most accomplished baritone that was ever in this country (and at this time a member of the Opera troupe), said to me, one evening, that he would be much pleased to hear my daughter sing, as he had heard from several of his friends that she possessed a very fine voice. I told him to name any afternoon or evening to call at my house, and she would sing for him with pleasure, for she had been more than delighted in hearing his performances at the opera for the past three or four months. He made the appointment to call the next day, and, according to promise, he presented himself in company with the conductor of the opera. They had never been introduced until now, but knew each other perfectly well, as they saw each other nightly. She told him at once that she would sing for him with great pleasure. She regretted that her old accompanist on the piano was not present, as it distracted her mind somewhat to accompany herself. She then took her seat at the piano (I will here remark by-the-by that she never sang to the wall, but had the instrument so placed as to face her listeners). She now asked Badialli from what opera she should sing, as she was well versed in most of the modern operas. He had no choice, she must choose for herself. She then commenced an aria from the opera of "Romeo and Juliet." She had not sung a dozen notes before he sprang to his feet, his eyes rolling like fireballs, he crossed the room to her and almost embraced her, and then paid her this compliment: "I have heard all the best and finest voices in Europe for thirty-five years, but never heard one to excel yours. Were you my daughter I would take you to London and Paris, and realize out of your voice $100,000 every six months." He appeared wild with delight, and said, "I will sing for you all night." In the course of further conversation he remarked to my daughter: "You know we played the opera of 'Ernani' last night, and I want you to sing with me the duet in the first act which I sing with the prima donna." She replied, "I know the music, but never had any one to sing it with." He replied, "You can sing any-thing." They commenced the duet and sang it through with as much apparent ease as if they had each been accustomed to sing it together for years. He then sang, as if with a spirit inspired, some of his gems from the different operas, and thus passed a most delightful and pleasant after-noon. In less than three months from the day of the occurrence I have just narrated, I conveyed her to my vault in Greenwood Cemetery.

She died very suddenly at Cozzen's Hotel, West Point, on the 31st of August, 1851, of congestion of the brain, sur-rounded, in her last hours, by other mem-bers of my family who had been spend-ing the summer there. Although dead twenty-three years I mourn her loss to this day, for she contributed so much to my happiness, during her short life of twenty-one years.

The advent of Jenny Lind, many years ago, on the concert stage created here a very great sensation, as she came heralded by a great European reputation. She and her company had been engaged by Barnum, the great showman. She possessed a magnificent musical organ, soprano in quality, with which she delighted her audiences. I attended all the concerts she gave in this city. It was truly delightful to hear her sing, and I listened to her as to the warbling of a beautiful bird, but she never reached my heart and soul; to me she did not possess that magic quality of sympathy that diffuses itself throughout the very soul and body; in short, she was not a Malibran. I had many disputes, and almost quarrels, with some of my musical friends on this very subject, but at length they partly yielded to my opinions and said I was probably right.

Some few years after Jenny Lind's appearance here, the world-renowned artists;

Grisi and Mario arrived. Grisi had been for a number of years the acknowledged star of the lyric stage, and Mario had no rival as a tenor in the European capitals; consequently their arrival here created great pleasure among our music-loving citizens. Grisi had passed her most brilliant days, and was rather passé; but she was a magnificent artist, both in singing and acting; you lost her identity in the character she represented. Mario was in the noontide of his musical powers; as an actor he was tame, but his splendid voice fully overcame his deficiency in that respect. They had a splendid success. I attended every one of their performances in this city.

I have omitted to give my recollections of the second Italian opera company that arrived in this city. The then principal performers were Montressor, tenor; Tonisario, basso-baritone; and Pedotte, soprano. The three constituted a splendid trio.

Rapetti, the celebrated violinist, was the leader of the orchestra. They opened at the Richmond Hill Theatre, corner of Charlton and Varick Streets (the ground upon which this theatre stood was formerly the country seat of Aaron Burr). They performed with great success to full houses for two or three months, and were liberally rewarded. The popularity of this company was the cause of the erection of a new opera-house on the corner of Church and Leonard Streets. In the meantime an agent was dispatched to Europe to engage an Italian company for the new house.

In due time the house was finished, and the new Italian company arrived, and soon after commenced their performances. They all, with one exception, the prima donna soprano, were second-rate performers, and it was not possible for one fine voice alone to sustain the company for any length of time, and it was finally disbanded.

Some time later we had an English opera company arrive here, consisting of Mr. and Mrs. Seguin, Mr. Wilson, Miss Sheriff, and Miss Poole, which formed the best English troupe that had ever been in this country before or since. They performed to delighted audiences for a long time, and the writer, with his daughters, was present at most of the performances.

Many years after the Astor Place Opera-house was erected by Mr. Morgan, by subscription for five years, each subscriber paying $300 a year in advance, which entitled him to three seats for the season. When the house was finished the seats were distributed by lot to the subscribers. When my name was drawn I chose the second sofa in the stage-box, which contained four seats, which added one more to my annual subscription, but which I retained for the five years. During those five years of Italian opera the managers had varied successes and drawbacks, and

frequently the five-year subscribers were
called upon to advance means to pay the
salaries of the performers, when the treas-
ury was empty; for it depended on the
subscribers, under adverse circumstances,
whether the house should be closed and
the opera suspended. In one of these di-
lemmas a meeting of the subscribers was
called, and it was voted that money enough
should be subscribed, and the number of
operas advertised to be given for the season should all be performed. This was
done, and, if my memory serves me cor-
rectly, I think I paid about $250 extra,
during the five years, to keep the opera
going.

During a greater portion of the time we
had a splendid collection of artists and
stars of the first magnitude, that from time
to time graced the stage. We had Salvi,
a tenor, one of the finest voices I ever
heard, besides he was a splendid actor,
and his voice very sympathetic; we had

Badialli (of whom I have before spoken),
the best baritone I ever heard; we had
also Tedesco and Bosio for sopranos, a portion of the time, each of them elegant vo-
calists, who performed to full and delighted
audiences for two or three months; we had
Marino, a basso, with great power as well
as a splendid performer; also Beneventano,
a very good baritone; and we had numerous other artists of greater or less celebrity.   Madame Patti and her husband,
the parents of the celebrated Patti, who
has been abroad so many years, the brilliant and universally admired prima donna,
in all the capitals of Europe.   She is said
to have no rivals in her own rôles.   Her
mother had a very high soprano voice of
fine quality, and I distinctly recollect her as
Juliet, in the opera of " Romeo and Juliet,"
in which character she was very celebrated.
Her husband was stage-manager, and occasionally took second-rate . characters in
the opera.   The chorus were well drilled,

and gave universal satisfaction. The authors of the leading operas performed were Rossini, Donizetti, and Bettini. Rossini's opera of the "Barber of Seville," I have heard sung over one hundred times. It was always a great favorite with the lovers of music. As I have said before, it was the first opera performed by the Garcia troupe, at the old Park Theatre, and I can almost listen even now, in imagination, to that magnificent voice of the daughter (afterwards Malibran), although forty years have passed away.

In this connection I will relate a little anecdote of Sontag and Malibran, those two great artists. This was related to me by Mr. Charles E. Horn, the English tenor, some thirty years ago. "They were both engaged at the London Italian opera. 'Norma' was performed one evening, in which each had a rôle, the one in the character of 'Norma,' and the other as 'Adelgisa.' There is in that opera one of the most beautiful duets ever written by man, and sung by these two great artists; there was a magic inspiration that seemed to pervade each of them in the execution of this beautiful duet. At its close they involuntarily threw themselves into each other's arms and embraced each other, apparently ignoring the presence of the audience; each had imparted to the other the magic influence of their mutual glorious execution, and the sympathetic influence of each filled their own souls with joy and delight. They imparted to their audience the same electric thrill that agitated their own souls, and it is needless to say that (when free breathing was restored) the audience demanded the duet to be repeated."

Song, in its legitimate sense, is an attribute of the Deity, for we read in the Scriptures of the songs of the Heavenly Hosts, and I doubt not that the music of the upper sanctuary will form a portion of the ecstatic joys of Heaven.

6

I had forgotten to mention the first regular Italian opera company that ever sung in this city. Palmo, an Italian, who had been a long resident here, and who kept a very respectable restaurant in Broadway (just below the old City Hospital), had a great taste for the music of his native country, and with the assistance of a few of his countrymen succeeded in obtaining a lease of the small theatre in Chambers Street, then directly opposite the site where the new Court-House now stands, and shortly after opened it with Italian opera. The company selected were very good artists, but not of the highest rank. I only recollect the names of some three or four of the principal artists. Benedetti, the tenor; Beneventano, the baritone; and Barilla, soprano. It was a very respectable company, and was well equipped with a good orchestra and chorus. It was very well supported for some time, but at length the expenses of the establishment overbalanced the receipts, and poor Palmo had finally to give up the house and disband his company; and it was currently reported that he lost all his previous savings in this enterprise. I was a regular attendant at this house, from its commencement to its close.

Malibran possessed an indomitable will, and was very self-reliant, and knowing full well her powers to command, she never failed to put them into practice, when the occasion occurred, which very often happened, and she invariably came forth victorious. I had forgotten to mention that during her residence in this city, she was invited by the Rev. Dr. Wainwright, of Grace Church (then on the corner of Broadway and Rector Street), to sing one Sunday morning in connection with the choir attached to his church. (I would here remark that Dr. Wainwright was, some years later, made Bishop of this diocese.) Malibran kindly accepted the doctor's invitation. Dr. Wainwright was a great lover of music, and he frequently attended the musical entertainments I so often gave at my own house on Washington Square, consequently I became quite intimately acquainted with him. I was duly informed by the doctor, and some other of my musical friends, of the day she was to sing at Grace Church, and it is needless to say that I repaired to the church at an early hour of the morning, flushed with high expectations of enjoying a great musical treat. Nor was I disappointed. In the course of the morning service she sang from the sublime oratorio of Handel, the solo, "I know that my Redeemer liveth." There was a hushed and solemn awe that seemed to pervade the whole congregation during the exquisite and masterly execution of that glorious gem of music. It was a day long to be remembered by the true lovers of music who were present on that occasion. I had repeatedly heard the same solo sung by many superior artists, but Malibran far excelled them all.

THE EUTERPIAN SOCIETY.

I will now say a few words regarding one of our old musical societies—the Euterpian. It was purely instrumental. It has for many years ceased to exist. I believe every member is now dead, except Mr. Contoit and myself. It met once a month, fifty years ago, on the corner of Fulton and Nassau Streets, and twenty years later at Riley's Tavern, in West Broadway. The society gave a public concert once a year at the old City Hotel, and after the concert a ball; and while this was in progress the old members had a supper below. It was one of the events of the season, and the assembly-room was always crowded on the occasion. Samuel B. Romaine, Esq., was one of its last presidents. I can now recollect only a few of its prominent members—John McKay, J. Westervelt, and Mr.

Earl, the former the organist, and the latter the leader of the choir in the old Dutch Church in Nassau Street, now occupied as the New York Post-office. Mr. Lamaire, Mr. Kyle, Mr. Contoit, of ice-cream memory, and many others whose names I have forgotten.

TEDESCO.

It was quite early in the history of the introduction of Italian opera into this city that a vessel arrived here from Havana, consigned to the old firm of Spofford, Tileston & Co., which had on board an Italian company of artists, who had been singing there to the close of their engagement. This company came consigned, in some measure, to the above firm, for an introduction to some of our music-loving people. In the afternoon of the day on which they arrived, young Mr. Spofford called at my office and requested the privilege of introducing me to the prima donna of the company, knowing me to take great interest in all musical matters. I accepted his invitation, and proposed meeting him at the Astor House, where the troupe were stopping, at five o'clock that afternoon.

We met accordingly, and he soon dispatched a servant to advise the lady that he had a musical friend with him, whom he wished to introduce. A few moments later a reply came that she was sick and in her bed. I then said I would call in the morning at ten o'clock, and was about leaving when another message came saying the lady would receive us. Without more ado Mr. Spofford and myself were conducted to her chamber. An elderly lady was standing beside the bed, who was introduced as the mother of the prima donna, while the young lady made an apology, saying she had taken cold and had concluded to nurse herself well of it. This was my introduction to Tedesco. We spent a short time in a pleasant and agreeable conversation, in which she told me she had letters of introduction to Mr. Simpson, then manager of the Park Theatre, whom she would see in the morning, and hoped to arrange with him for a short engagement. I promised to call on her the next day, and that she could command my services to assist her, as far as it was in my power to do so. I called on her the following day, and was most graciously received, when she informed me that she had seen Mr. Simpson, and had arranged for a short season of opera, to commence the following week. I expressed my pleasure at this good news, and told her I should go at once and secure five seats for each night of her performances.

The opening night at length came, the theatre was well filled, and the opera was "Ernani." The cavatina in the first act was her opening song. Her appearance on the stage created a sensation throughout the house, for she had a most commanding presence, and was withal a very handsome woman. When her first beautiful notes were heard there were such thunders of applause that her fame as a vocalist was as firmly established as the ground we tread upon, and she continued to gain fresh laurels from all her future performances.

At the close of the engagement here, the troupe went to Boston, where she received the same admiration and applause that was bestowed upon her here. During her engagement there I visited Boston with some members of my family, and we attended the opera every evening during our stay there. It might almost be supposed that the magnet of attraction was the opera that drew me there; be it so, but I associated with it a little business transaction that could have been postponed to a later period without suffering loss by the delay.

6*

CHAPTER XIII.

MEMBERS OF THE PRODUCE EXCHANGE.

THE first idea that now occurs to me are the most prominent merchants of our Produce Exchange. I am the oldest member, and when I first went on 'Change, some fifty-five years ago, our meeting was at the old Tontine building, corner of Wall and Water Streets. There were, comparatively, few brokers in the produce line in those days, and the floor of that Exchange was mostly devoted to many of our principal shipping merchants; and the few produce brokers, who attended regularly, had the opportunity of making the acquaintance of those merchants, and the more industrious of us soon acquired a thriving business from them.

Some years later the Exchange on Wall Street was built, and we removed to more commodious quarters in that building; in the meantime our numbers were largely increased, and we remained there until the great fire that burned the lower part of our city, including our Exchange. From thence we removed to the lofts of two large buildings in Broad Street, procured for that purpose by a committee of our Board, and remained there until the enlarged Exchange on Wall Street was rebuilt. Here we remained until the Government purchased the building for the Custom House; we then procured the building corner of Broad and South Streets, with the two adjoining ones on South and Broad Streets, and, with some alterations, it made rather a convenient place for the meeting of our members.

Some two or three years later the property on which stands our present Exchange was purchased, and as soon as the present building was erected, we removed to it and still remain there. It is now proposed, however, by some of our members that some other location further up-town be procured for the erection of a still larger building, as many complain that the present one is overcrowded. Whether this project will be put in execution at an early day is to my mind very uncertain.

The most prominent members of our Exchange at the present time are David Dows & Co., Jesse Hoyt & Co., Armour, Plankinton & Co., Cragin & Co., Kent & Co., Isaac H. Reed & Co., Jewell, Harrison & Co., Ward, Foster & Co., Brush & Co., Sawyer, Wallace & Co., J. M. Requa & Co., Cooper & Co., Colgate & Co., B. W. Floyd, William Moses, Tompkins & Co., Work, Pennell & Foster, J. W. McCulloh, Woodruff & Robinson, Gould, H. Thorp, and over two thousand other subscribers, with the larger proportion of whom I am totally unacquainted; but besides the twenty firms above-named there are doubtless hundreds of others equally prominent and as highly respected as those I have mentioned. I beg here to remark that the two first named are said to be the wealthiest members of the Exchange.

The largest importers of teas, raw silks, etc., for many years past, is the old house of A. A. Low & Brothers. Some few years ago they had ten or eleven vessels in the China trade, now they have but three or four. The importation of teas, for two or three years past, has been unprofitable. In fact, Mr. Lyman, for many years a prominent member of this house, told me, some time ago, that they were then selling teas at a loss of ten cents a pound, and hence the sale of their vessels.

The Suez Canal, since its opening to navigation, has been one of the principal sources through which teas have been imported to this country. The time between the shipment at the Chinese ports to this country does not average one-half as much as compared with the old route. For many years I have been intimately acquainted with Mr. Lyman, and have had large transactions with the house in supplying their vessels with stores and cargo. This firm has a reputation for integrity, honesty, and liberality in all their transactions that will favorably compare with any other large house in this country. It always gives me pleasure to testify to the worth of a house so universally respected.

In this connection I must say a few words in relation to the old firm of Suydam, Sage & Co., who did a very large commission business in this city for a number of years, and with whom I had large business transactions. Mr. Suydam died many years ago, but the business of the old firm continued with Mr. Sage and one or two of Mr. Suydam's sons. Mr. Sage died several years ago, leaving a family of sons and daughters and his widowed wife.

May 15, 1874.—There was a banquet given at Delmonico's last evening by a number of the younger members of the Exchange. I was specially invited to attend. I was compelled to decline the kind invitation for the following reasons: For the past six months I have not left my lodgings after dark; besides, my age admonishes me that if I wish to retain my present good health, I must avoid all crowded assemblies, where mirth, merriment, and the flowing bowl circulate freely. Thus I am often compelled to deny myself the pleasures of an hour, lest that hour might be the cause of days, and perhaps weeks, of regret and suffering. I was pleased to hear on 'Change to-day from several of the members, who attended the festival last evening, that everything passed off very pleasantly and agreeably to the company present.

CHAMBER OF COMMERCE AND OLD MERCHANTS.

I have just returned to my office from the rooms of the Chamber of Commerce, it being their monthly meeting for the transaction of business, as also the day for the election of officers for the ensuing year. This day is the hundredth year of its first organization, and is to be celebrated this evening with a banquet at Delmonico's. I am the oldest living member on its rolls.

There were several important old firms in this city, now extinct, with whom I had large business transactions. N. L. & G. Griswold, G. G. & S. Howland (afterwards Howland & Aspinwall); the younger branches of this house still remain under the last-named firm. Spofford & Tileston, a most enterprising firm, established themselves many years ago and were wonderfully successful, and they certainly merited the wealth they acquired. In the mercan tile community no name stood higher than theirs. Mr. Tileston was, for many years, president of the Phœnix Bank.

CHAPTER XIV.

THE GREAT FIRE OF 1835.

I RESIDED in Cortlandt Street at the time of the occurrence of this dreadful calamity. During the evening I had been attending a lecture at the Mercantile Library, then located in Beekman Street, opposite the Old Brick Church. I was, at this time, a stockholder in this institution. If my memory is not at fault, it was shortly before nine o'clock when the fire-alarm first sounded. It was a bitter cold night. Very great was my surprise the next morning in going to my store, to discover the awful ravages it had made from Wall Street to Coenties Slip. All the principal buildings within this space on Wall, South, Front, Water, and Pearl Streets had been destroy-

ed. It was a smouldering mass of ruins.
When I reached my store I found the fire
had not crossed Coenties Slip on the lower
side, but it was believed by many that it
would, and I at once made arrangements to
remove my stock of goods to the Battery,
and had all my cartmen and workmen
ready on the spot for that purpose, but
fortunately I was not molested by it.

The greater portion of that day I spent
in visiting the ruin and havoc it had made.
The scene was most truly a melancholy
one, but in a comparatively short time the
débris of the burnt district was removed,
and new stores immediately erected; and in
many locations property advanced more
than to cover the cost of erecting new
buildings. In fact, the losses sustained by
our merchants was in the loss of their
destroyed goods, which in many instances
would have amounted to nothing had not
most of our insurance companies become
so crippled that they were unable to pay.

It is truly a matter of wonder and surprise to see how soon after great fires have de-vastated our large cities, how they spring, like the fabled phœnix, from their ashes! It truly may be said we are a go-ahead people. We do our business rapidly and quickly, without any loss of time.

There are but few of the old landmarks remaining to tell the present generation what New York was seventy-six years ago. No. 1 Broadway is said to have been built one hundred and seventeen years ago. The brick was imported from Holland, and the building was probably looked upon, in those early days, as a model of everything desirable in the way of architecture and comfort; but the building has been almost entirely remodelled. The old building on the corner of Broad and Pearl Streets is another old-time association of this city; it has been kept for several years as a public house. The next old landmark is the Walton House, in Pearl Street, oppo-

site Harper & Brothers' publishing house.
There may be a few other old landmarks
about the city, but I doubt if any can claim
the same age as those I have mentioned.
The city of New York has been built over
two or three times during the past eighty
or ninety years. And the immense rise in
real estate, during the past twenty-five
years, warrants all the improvements that
have taken place in that period.

CROTON WATER—INTRODUCTION TO NEW YORK.

The celebration on the occasion of the
introduction of the Croton water into our
city, many years ago, will long be remembered. The procession on this occasion
was the most imposing and magnificent I
ever beheld. All the mechanical arts were
represented — the different trades, and,
taken altogether, it was an outburst of joy
at the completion of this great work ; and

how thankful we should be for the great benefits we have derived from it, but the great majority do not think of the inestimable blessing it has conferred. The day was observed throughout the city as a general holiday, business was almost entirely suspended, and every one seemed to rejoice that this great work was finished. It requires a pen greatly superior to mine to paint and portray the glowing scenes of that day; but the present generation cannot fully appreciate the joy and gladness that thrilled our souls at the prospect hereafter of drinking from God's pure fountain the pure water of life.

To Mr. Van Schaick, more than any other man, was this city indebted for the early introduction of the Croton water. He was one of its directors and president of the board, and exerted all his powers, and gave all his time, to the task that devolved upon him. I was personally acquainted with Mr. Van Schaick (formerly one of the part-

ners of the house of John & Philip Hone),
and although we differed in politics I always gave him my vote whenever he was
'a candidate for any municipal office, for I
esteemed him highly, and knew him to be
a strictly honest man.

OUR MARKETS.

In regard to the early markets of this
city there was one in Broad Street in 1800,
between Water and South Streets, but my
memory is at fault when it was demolished.
It remained only a few years. There was
another one in Maiden Lane at the same
time, in 1800, commencing at Broadway
and running down some distance; but
again I am at a loss to know when this
was demolished. The old Fly Market, in
Maiden Lane, ran from Pearl Street to the
East River. This was one of the largest
and most prominent of any in the city. It
remained a number of years on that site,
and was finally demolished, and the present

Fulton Market erected in its stead. The present Washington Market was first erected in Greenwich Street, and some years after re-built on its present site, and enlarged from time to time. The Catharine Street Market was built previous to my residence in the city, in 1798, and it still remains, with some additions. The next in importance was the Canal Street Market, foot of Spring and Canal Streets, but I cannot give the date when it was erected.

There are many others in the upper portion of the city that I have never seen, but I did not purpose when I commenced these papers to give any description of the rapid growth and extension of the city for the past thirty-five years, with the exception of a few of the more important erections of mammoth structures of recent dates, well knowing that the present generation are better posted than myself in regard to the rapid growth of our city. There are numerous portions of it I have never seen, and there are hundreds of extensive manufactories whose doors I have never entered. The Jefferson Market, on Sixth Avenue, between Eighth and Ninth Streets, I patronized during my residence on Washington Square (twenty-nine years). I am not posted when that market was built.

7

CHAPTER XV.

PUBLIC MEN.

I HAVE always considered Clay and Webster the two great intellectual giants in the Senate of the United States, and, in my opinion, we have had nothing to equal them since their day. When Mr. Clay was running for President, in opposition to Polk, I gave the old Whig committee $200 to add to the fund for the support of Mr. Clay; but he was defeated by jugglery and corruption. In my early manhood I resided for many years in the Seventh Ward, and regularly attended the Whig ward meetings, and for three or four years was regularly nominated the secretary of these meetings. At this period ·we had no printed ballots; they were all written, and for two or three days previous to the election I employed most of my time in writing out ballots for distribution; but I beg here to say that I never applied for any political office in my life. My business absorbed all my time, as I have said before. I have been a regular business merchant for over sixty years, and during that period, say from thirty to thirty-five years, my average income was more than the salary of the President of the United States. I have always paid one hundred cents on the dollar for every purchase I ever made, which has amounted to many millions during my lifetime. This fact gives me more comfort and pleasure in my old age than all the gold in Wall Street, particularly as no portion of it was obtained by fraud or dishonesty. I never was a worshipper of the almighty dollar, but I took much pleasure in making it honestly.

During the period of my prosperity in business I kept horses and carriages, more

particularly for the benefit and pleasure of
my family, for I cared but little for riding,
and did not drive out of the city for pleasure three times a year. I had my wagon,
which was always ordered to be at my door
every morning, and after taking breakfast
I would call on my numerous customers
around the city, and drive from thence to my
store on Front Street, where I discharged
my coachman, with orders to wait on my
family for the remainder of the day. During the time of my large and prosperous
business I was in the habit of returning
home at from four to five o'clock, and dining
at six o'clock, with my mind freed from
all business cares, and devoted. my even-
ings, four or five of them weekly, to the
Opera and other musical entertainments,
in which I so much delighted.

GENERAL JACKSON.

After the close of the war of 1812 General Jackson visited this city, and in his

honor a public dinner was given at Tammany Hall. I was one of the many who attended it. The tickets were $5. At this time there was a great division in the Democratic ranks between De Witt Clinton and Daniel D. Tompkins, the greater portion favoring the latter. When the General was called on for his toast, he gave "De Witt Clinton, Governor of the State of New York." At this announcement a large portion of the guests dropped their heads as if thunderstruck. The evening passed away, however, very pleasantly, with music, songs, and wine, and at a somewhat late hour we all retired, well pleased with the evening's entertainment. As I have before said, I will here again remark, that I was never a Democrat, but always a Whig in those days of the Clay and Webster school. I always voted against every Democratic candidate for the Presidency, Andrew Jackson included.

CHAPTER XVI.

THE YOUNG MEN FORMERLY IN MY EMPLOY.

I NOW propose to speak of the young men who were in my employ many years ago, and it gives me great pleasure to record the many sterling qualities they possessed, without arrogating to myself any credit for the instructions given to these boys. I refer to them as men and merchants, whether I ever failed by example or precept from giving them aught but good advice. I endeavored to instil into their minds that honesty was the true policy; and, all other considerations aside, this noble truth will abide all consequences and will remain forever—that an honest man is the noblest work of God.

My first clerk was William C. Dougherty,

who remained with me some fifteen years, and the latter portion of his time I gave him an interest in my business; he was a man of strict integrity. He left my concern many years ago, and established himself in business on his own account, in which he has prospered, and has taken rank on 'Change, for his honesty and industry, with the most prominent members of that institution.

Charles Fordham was the second boy I took into my office. With his father's family I was intimately acquainted. Some years ago he left me to seek his fortune in California. He was taken sick in San Francisco and died; he was a most excellent young man.

Theodore Johnson was the third young man I took in my employ; he remained with me a number of years. He was strictly honest and attentive to business, and commanded the universal respect of all who knew him.

Mr. Charles H. Johnson, brother of the former, was my fourth clerk, who remained in my office for many years. He was, like his brother, honest, industrious and intelligent, and respected by all who knew him. He attends our Produce Exchange daily, and is a highly respectable member.

John Dougherty, my fifth clerk, who is a nephew of William C. Dougherty, my first, came into my office at the age of seventeen years and remained until he was twenty one. He was, like my other clerks, honest, industrious, and attentive to business; he also is a daily attendant on the Exchange, and occupies there a highly respectable position.

My sixth clerk was a brother of my two former clerks named Johnson. I can scarcely recollect him, for shortly after he came with me he was taken ill and died suddenly.

In referring to the clerks I have brought up in my office I am not unmindful of the services of gentlemen who rendered me great service during my business career. I allude to the different bookkeepers I have had in my employ. There must necessarily be a distinction between the young men I took in my employ and those who came with me as accomplished accountants. I never had cause to find the first fault with any of them.

In the past forty years, five have been in my employ, and, with the exception of Mr. Pollock, who was the last I employed, they are all dead. But I desire here to say of this gentleman, that no one in my employ gave me greater satisfaction.

I allude to them all, with that certain knowledge I possess, that they were gentlemen of integrity and character; and in paying this little tribute of regard to my old bookkeepers, I have felt it a duty to connect their names with the other clerks I employed.

7*

CHAPTER XVII.

CENTRAL PARK.

THERE have never been two acts of incorporation for our city of which I am so proud, and for which I used all the influence I possessed so perseveringly, as for the Croton water and the Central Park. Of the former, it was almost my daily advocacy for two or three years before the final act of incorporation. The cost was the great bugbear with many of our citizens, while I scouted the cost at any figures, however large, declaring I was willing to pay $500 a year for its use sooner than not obtain it. Croton water has been my constant and daily beverage since its introduction, and I have no doubt it has been the cause of adding many. years. to my. prolonged life. Previous to its introduction I bought water for drinking purposes, and used my well water for other domestic uses, and for my stable. I have ever esteemed it one of the greatest blessings ever conferred on this city; but the present generation cannot fully appreciate its worth, for they never knew its loss.

Central Park was the next great blessing to our city, for which I was a strenuous advocate. I have watched its incipient beginning up to the present day, and feel proud of its advancement to its present condition. Its drives and walks are unsurpassed; its bridges and ornamentations are substantial and beautiful; its lakes, with the surrounding scenery, are very interesting; the shady walks in the Ramble are delightful, while the general outline of the Park is ornamented with numerous rustic bowers. In addition to all these attractions, there are vastly more important facts relating to the influence the Park presents to the poorer classes of our citizens, many of whom were in the habit of spending their Sundays in dram-shops before the opening of this magnificent work, and who now go regularly with their families, providing themselves with the necessaries to spend the greater portion of the day; hence they commingle with the more respectable classes of society, and this, no doubt, has had a great influence on many who had been (as before said) in the habit of passing the day so very differently.

The largest and most substantial work in the Park is the Terrace, at the head of the Mall, near the large fountain and the lake. It is the decided gem of the Park, most elaborately adorned with carvings by the best artists in this country, and is actually a study and delight to those who have a taste for sculpture to critically examine it. This work is said to have cost half a million of dollars. The interior, during the spring and summer, is used as a restaurant, the ceiling of which is a per-

fect gem of art, and cannot fail of strik
ing the most indifferent visitor with wonder and delight. I have examined it
time and again with renewed pleasure.
There is another building on the north
side of the Park, erected for soda-water
fountains, very unique in its architecture
and proportions, and highly ornamented.
The old Arsenal appears of late to be
the great centre of attraction for a large
proportion of the visitors, many of them
thinking this more interesting than any
other portion of the Park, with its mu-
seum of wild animals, birds and a thousand other curiosities too numerous to mention. When I go to the Park I always
stop at the Casino, where I usually take an
ice-cream and a lemonade. The proprietors of the Casino I have been personally
acquainted with for many years. They
are both highly respectable gentlemen.
The two largest reservoirs of the Croton
are in this Park, while the distributing res-

ervoir is on Murray Hill, which supplies all the lower portion of the city. There are many interesting points in the upper portion of the Park which I have not visited for two years past, and during that time further improvements have doubtless been made in beautifying the grounds in that portion. What would our citizens do in their leisure hours without the pleasures arising from their drives, or rambles on foot, through Central Park? There is one important carving (I forgot to mention) near the Casino, of two figures carved in stone, illustrating a social scene in the life of Robert Burns the poet, which thousands of our citizens stop to admire; it illustrates a scene from his "Tam o' Shanter and Souter Johnny," and was executed by one of the workmen employed on the Park, who also executed a portion of the carvings on the Terrace.

The new Post-Office, now in course of completion in the City Hall Park, is a mag-

nificent building, as well as an ornament to
our city. I well recollect, fifty-five years
ago, when our city Post-Office was on the
corner of William and Garden Streets, now
Exchange Place. Mr. Bailey was then
Postmaster. At that period I paid $3 a
year for my private box. I now pay $16,
but the increase in this particular is not
more than the increase for other necessaries.

CHAPTER XVIII.

THE OLD ARISTOCRACY.

SEVENTY years ago there were many more aristocratic families in this city than there are at the present time. There were then quite a large number of the old Knickerbockers who have passed away during the past two generations. I can distinctly remember the names of many of them—the Livingstons, the Bayards, the Kings, the Gracies, the Varicks, the Osgoods, the McEvers, the Van Rensselaers, the Primes, and many others I cannot call to mind. They were in the habit of giving, two or three times a year, dancing assemblies at the old City Hotel. The company was very exclusive, and it was difficult for an outsider to gain admittance, except

highly recommended by some of the managers. There was much etiquette observed
at their assemblies, particularly so when any
new members were first introduced. That
generation has mostly passed away, and
two new generations have succeeded them,
who have principally been the architects
of their own fortunes, and many of them
have attained to great wealth—some of
them, whose ancestors were from the lowest grades of society; but great credit is
due to those who sprung from poverty to
independence. The present test of society
is he who can wield the largest purse. At
this time the almighty dollar covers a mul
titude of sins, and is the idol which thousands worship.

It may appear somewhat invidious, in
writing my own biography in connection
with incidents appertaining to this city
seventy years ago, to speak in praise of my
own ancestry, but when given strictly in
truth and sincerity, without any prevarica

tion whatever, I feel certainly justified in
so doing, and, as before observed, of my
ancestry both on my father's and mother's
side I feel very proud, and would to God I
had inherited all their virtues.

PETER COOPER, ETC.

There is a name that will go down to
posterity ranking with the greatest philanthropists of the age.   I allude to Mr. Peter
Cooper. Perhaps there is no one man in
this city who has so largely contributed, by
his acts of benevolence, to ameliorate the
condition of our worthy poor by providing
instruction in various branches of knowledge, particularly scientific, by which they
will be enabled to earn a respectable living.   Mr. Cooper is entitled to the thanks
of every citizen of this city, and I would
rather be the wearer of the garland that is
gathering upon his brow than the crown of
any monarch upon earth; for the latter will
soon perish with its using, while the gar-

land will grow more and more beautiful for ages to come. And may the Cooper Institute continue to flourish and communicate instruction to thousands of the present and rising generations, and may its name live for generations to come in the grateful recollection of their friend and benefactor.

The present century has been one in which science has reached the most brilliant results. The application of steam to all the industries in mechanical operations of the day, but more particularly to the propelling power of our marine, is unprecedented in any former age of the world. The ocean is now literally covered with thousands of steamers which navigate every portion of our globe, and we have been so accustomed to see them arrive and depart, that we hardly realize the inestimable benefits arising from this great invention.

In my estimation, the electric telegraph far surpasses any former achievement of man in the sciences. The utmost stretch of the powers of man cannot describe or tell us the causes, why or wherefore, a message sent over the electric wire three thousand miles, either under water or overland, will reach its destination in two or three minutes. It is altogether incomprehensible, it cannot be explained; although the facts are plain and positive, it is miraculous and almost strikes me as being a spark from the Divinity itself, and guided by the same Divine power. "There is a limit across which man cannot carry any one of its conceptions, and from the ulterior of which he cannot gather a single ray of light to guide or inform him." The above quotation in some measure illustrates the workings of that mysterious power connected with the electric telegraph which defies both time and space. Suffice it to say, the names of Fulton and Morse will go down to posterity with accumulated blessings and honor for all time to come.

JOHN JACOB ASTOR.

John Jacob Astor occupied a high position for wealth during the early part of my business career. He then resided in Broadway, on the site of the present Astor House, in a large fifty feet front house, while his business office was in the rear, on Vesey Street, where he sold his furs. I believe the present generation are fully aware that from his extensive dealings in furs he laid the foundation of his enormous fortune. He was the owner of the Park Theatre, and I occasionally went there in my younger days, and I always saw the old gentleman there in his private box, which was located at the end of the orchestra through the pit entrance. One might moralize on the life and death of such a man; his accumulation of millions upon millions are of no more avail to him now than to the poorest who sleep near his grave—in this one respect they are equal.

Mr. Astor entered largely into real estate at an early day, and his heirs are undoubtedly the largest real estate owners in this country.

COLONEL HENRY RUTGERS.

When my father first removed to this city in 1798, he located his family in the Seventh Ward, first in Cheapside Street, then in Henry, and at length in Rutgers Street. Colonel Rutgers lived three or four blocks above Rutgers Street; the grounds about his house occupied an entire block. He was then one of the most prominent men of the day. He possessed an immense landed estate of several thousands of lots in the immediate neighborhood of his private dwelling. He was never married; he was most highly respected by all who knew him. He was a quiet and unostentatious man. In addition to these qualities he was very charitable, and distributed his large wealth with a liberal hand.

He gave the ground on which the Rutgers Street Presbyterian Church now stands, and contributed largely to the means for the erection of the church. His nephew, Mr. William B. Crosby, was his sole agent in superintending his large estate, renting and collecting his revenues. Mr. Crosby was the father of the Rev. Dr. Howard Crosby, and the present Chancellor of the New York University. Colonel Rutgers left to his nephew a large property.

My removal so many years ago from that portion of the city has left me totally ignorant of the then rising population, and the Crosbys, as well as many other families with whom I was formerly acquainted, have passed from my memory like a morning dream. After the death of Colonel Rutgers, Mr. Crosby and family occupied the premises for many years, until the growth and extension of business compelled him to dispose of his property for business purposes, and the entire grounds were converted into stores, where the busy population of to-day are applying their vocation in the once peaceful and quiet home of its former occupants.

My sister (Mrs. Wilkie) resided opposite Colonel Rutgers for many years, and their families were intimately acquainted.

CHAPTER XIX.

CHURCHES.

In 1798 there were but three Presbyterian Churches in this city, namely—the Wall Street Church, the Brick Church, and the Rutgers Street Church. The officiating clergymen were the Rev. Dr. Rodgers, Rev. Dr. McKnight, and the Rev. Dr. Samuel Miller. They alternated weekly between the three. My father's family attended the Rutgers Street Church, and my father was for several years a ruling member or deacon. I heard the Rev. Dr. Miller preach the centennial sermon in 1800. I was then fifteen years of age. What vast changes since then! The number of Presbyterian Churches scattered throughout the city is almost incredible. During my

8

residence in Cortlandt Street I attended the Murray Street Church, the Rev. Dr. McAuley was then its pastor. In later years this church was sold and carefully taken down, and removed to Eighth Street, Dr. McAuley still retaining the pastorship. This church finally got into financial difficulties and was re-sold to Mr. A. T. Stewart. It still remains standing, and is now known as St. Ann's Catholic.

The clergymen who occupied the pulpits of the different churches named in this paper were men of mark. Of the three first named, Dr. Samuel Miller occupied the first rank in my opinion. During my residence on Washington Square I attended the Rev. Dr. Potts' church, who was a man of very superior talents, and gave universal satisfaction to his congregation. This church was located on the corner of Ninth Street and University Place.

ST. PAUL'S CHURCH, TRINITY, AND ST. JOHN'S.

St. Paul's Church is the oldest Episcopal edifice in this city. I distinctly recollect, on my first visit to New York, when I was not more than eight years of age, I was so fascinated (as young as I was) with the beautiful structure and its surroundings, that I often stopped and gazed on it with childish admiration and delight, for, of course, it was a perfect wonder to me, and I could scarcely believe that such immense buildings could be erected for church purposes, drawing the comparison between it and our plain meeting-houses in Orange County. Within a year or so this church has been entirely renovated in the interior, and it now presents itself, with its beautiful stained glass and many other improvements, as second to no church in this city, notwithstanding the many elegant ones that have been erected in the last few years in the upper part of the city.

George Washington worshipped in this church in his day, and I am told his initials were on one of the pews when it was renovated a few years ago. Old Trinity was demolished a great many years ago, and the present structure erected in its stead. It is useless to say that this building is simply magnificent. St. John's is the third which constituted what was then Trinity Parish. This church was erected many years after the two above-mentioned, and is a model of elegance and beauty; and may they all stand for ages to come to dispense those glorious truths, which, if practised and believed, will lead us all to immortality.

CLERGYMEN, ETC.

I am now going to allude to some of my favorite clergymen, and I will here re-mark, in this connection, that the Bible is my usual daily companion. In its teach-ings and inspirations I am a firm believer.

At the Presbyterian churches I attend regularly. Yesterday, March 22d, 1874, I heard Dr. Taylor in the morning. He took his text from Daniel, on the downfall and death of Belshazzar, at the great feast he gave his nobles at Babylon, when he ordered the sacred vessels of Jerusalem to be brought to him to add to the orgies and blasphemies of their drunken revels. Dr. Taylor drew many very interesting illustrations from his subject in relation to the temperance movements now pervading many portions of our country, and many of his remarks were not only sublime and thrilling, but withal very dramatic; in fact it was a regular temperance sermon, and most admirably delivered. In the afternoon I went to hear Dr. Booth, who delivered a very able discourse from St. John's gospel, on the suffering, death, and resurrection of our Saviour. May 17th, 1874.—Yesterday I again heard Dr. Taylor, who, to my mind, is one of the most interesting and eloquent of our divines. His text was, "What think ye of Christ?" After a few preliminary remarks he divided his discourse into four divisions First, those who believe Christ to be an impostor; second, those who believe Him to be a harmless, zealous individual; third, those who believe Him inspired with miraculous powers of doing good to his fellow-men, who disbelieve in His divine attributes with the Deity as being the Son of God; fourth, His logical and eloquent interpretation of the Scriptures, in which he proves conclusively the Trinity of the God-head—Father, Son, and Holy Ghost. It was truly a splendid exposition of Bible history, and must have carried conviction to every hearer. In the afternoon I attended my old Church, corner of Tenth Street and University Place, again to hear Dr. Booth, who gave his congregation a very interesting discourse, in which he remarked that that day twenty years ago he preached his first sermon in Auburn State Prison to a very different audience from the one he was then addressing.

May 24, 1874.—Since making a few remarks upon Mr. Beecher I have heard him preach. I went to his church yesterday. He took for his text the eighth verse of the second chapter of Paul's epistle to the Ephesians: "By grace are ye saved, through faith; and that not of yourselves, it is the gift of God." It was certainly the most logical sermon I ever heard, and many portions of it were beautifully illustrated. He has a very fine voice and distinct delivery, for there was scarcely a word I did not hear. To say I was pleased would scarcely convey my impressions; I was delighted. But, notwithstanding the pleasure derived from his discourse, honest opinion compels me to say that there are several clergymen of this city whose ministrations I should prefer to attend regularly than those of Mr. Beecher.

In this connection it has this moment occurred to me to speak of a celebrated divine, Rev. Dr. Learned, who visited this city some fifty years ago. He was from New Orleans, where he was settled over a Presbyterian church, and was idolized by his congregation. He was a young man of some twenty-six or twenty-eight years of age. During his visit here I heard him preach twice, once in Rutgers Street Church and again in Garden Street Church. In the latter his discourse was on the death and sufferings of our Saviour. It was, without any exception, the most brilliant piece of oratory I ever heard from mortal lips. He actually seemed inspired with a prophetic magical influence that caused the tears to flow "from eyes unused to weep." His glowing and beautiful description of the sufferings and death of our Saviour, in language unsurpassed by its diction and beauty, together with the magical tone of his voice, conspired to render it the most

beautiful display of pulpit oratory I ever
heard. His next discourse was in Rutgers
Street Church, directed more particularly
to the younger portion of the congregation.
I have had the four last words of that sermon impressed on my memory ever since,
namely, " Go if you dare." There is a volume of meaning in those words as connected with his discourse. He possessed
another remarkable trait ; his memory was
wonderful. The moment he took his text
he closed the book, with no scrap of paper
to indicate even the heads of his discourse.
I will relate the following anecdote in illustration of these facts, as well as the wonderful influence he possessed in his delivery.
While visiting some portion of the South,
he was invited to preach for one of his
clerical friends. On their way to the
church his friend handed him a note which
he asked him to read to the congregation
at the close of the service. He ran his
eyes over the note, and placed it in his

8

pocket. At the close of the service he repeated the contents of the note to the congregation. On his return home with his friend after church he said to him, "I must compliment you on the beautiful manner and style in which you announced the principal contents of the note I gave you. I should feel very proud could I have dictated so beautiful an address as you substituted for mine." At these remarks Dr. Learned turned to his friend and said, "In giving out your notice to your congregation I neither added to, nor subtracted a single word from the original you gave me." His friend could scarcely believe the fact. This goes to prove the wonderful power a cultivated and beautiful voice may have over an ordinary communication. This young clergyman died in New Orleans, two years after his return, of yellow fever.

In connection with the above little history there was another young clergyman of the Methodist denomination who visited

this country from England shortly before,
or a year or two later, named Somerville,
scarcely twenty-one years of age, who created a great sensation. He was a fluent
and beautiful speaker, with a countenance
more like that of a girl than a man. He at-
tracted large audiences from every denomination, and was constantly invited to preach
in their different pulpits. He delivered one
sermon in the Old North Dutch Church
(now used for our Post-Office) on a week
day. I went there to hear him and found the
church so crowded that I could not obtain
even standing-room. His popularity was
immense, and he created a great reforma-
tion in the Methodist churches, particularly with some of his fellow-clergymen,
who, previous to his advent here, had been
in the habit of exciting themselves in the
pulpit and fairly screaming to their hearers
and exciting them also to loud *Amens*, etc.,
and even disturbing the more quiet portion
of the congregation. Those sensational

preachers, who bellowed from their pulpits, miscalled it conversion-preaching; but the calm and beautiful discourses from the pure lips of Somerville soon had the desired effect of banishing from the Methodist pulpit the noisy preachers of that day. My memory does not serve me to say how long he remained in this city, but I believe about two years, and since his return to England I have no recollections of his after-life to record.

DRS. WAINWRIGHT AND POTTS.

In my previous remarks I have mentioned the names of Bishop Wainwright and the Rev. Dr. Potts. It may be remembered by some of our citizens that these two distinguished clergymen had a spirited newspaper discussion many years ago, Bishop Wainwright maintaining "that there could not be a church without a bishop," and Dr. Potts arguing in opposition. I have said that Dr. Wainwright was an enthusiastic ad-

mirer of music ; Dr. Potts was equally so.
He invariably sang with the choir of his
church, and had a very fine tenor voice. It
was on his ministrations that myself and
family attended during my residence on
Washington Square. He married two of my
youngest daughters, and he occasionally
dropped in at my musical entertainments.
In short, he was a most agreeable companion. My family and his were quite intimate.

REV. DR. HALL.

The Rev. Dr. Hall has been with us so
long that we may claim him as one of our
own people. His name and fame have become household words with us. Probably
no clergyman who ever visited this country
from the Old World has acquired so great
a popularity in so short a period of time as
Dr. Hall has. He appears to have identified
himself with every good work. At all the
charitable gatherings he has been a prompt
and willing advocate, and his addresses

before the different charitable societies of this city have had a great effect. There are few men who can give a telling speech on charity, but Dr. Hall appears to me to be most thoroughly qualified. May he long continue to be a blessing, not only to his large and devoted congregation, but also to the cause of charity and benevolence, as well as an illustration of all the Christian graces that adorn our humanity.

I often think of the thousands and tens of thousands who daily pass the grounds of Trinity and St. Paul's, if they ever give a thought to the thousands that lie beneath the sod. I fear not. The great mass, in passing and repassing, have their minds too much occupied with their different avocations to think, for a moment, that in a little while they must lay their bodies down to sleep, the same as those who now sleep there. Most of the old influential citizens of this city, fifty or sixty years ago, are there; a vast number of my old personal

friends lie there—the young and the old.
Here rest the remains of some of our great
heroes—Decatur, Lawrence, Kearney, and
others—and at the end may they all awake
to a bright resurrection beyond the grave,
to meet the heavenly hosts in everlasting
glory!

HENRY WARD BEECHER.

September 21st.—While on 'Change to-
day I was called upon by one of our old and
respected merchants to sign a document
signifying our belief as to the purity and
innocence of Mr. Beecher. The scandalous
charges that have been circulated against
this eminent man have filled my heart with
sorrow. I signed the paper cheerfully, for
I most honestly believe him guiltless of
the foul charges preferred against him.
The conspiracy to ruin him has been con-
cocted by a set of villains as base as ever
trod this footstool of God, and they richly
deserve the execrations of all mankind. I

am not personally acquainted with Mr. Beecher, but he has been so long in this community that his name has become a household word. His brilliant and beautiful discourses, with that ready display of oratory that he commands, will live in the hearts of many when he is gone.

CHAPTER XX.

WILLIAM B. COZZENS.

THERE never was in this country a more popular landlord than Mr. William B. Cozzens. He was admired and respected throughout our whole country, for everybody knew him. His elegant hotel at West Point is a model of everything that is beautiful. His tables were loaded with every delicacy known; and probably no hotel in this country was as much noted for its wines and liquors as his. He was particularly celebrated in his choice selection of wines, and he was considered a superior judge. I never spent my time more pleasantly than when at West Point. Mr.

Cozzens,* for many years, was the proprietor of the American Hotel, on the corner of Broadway and Barclay Street, and his 'house ranked as high as any in the city.

And I beg here to remark that, during the time Mr. Cozzens kept the American Hotel, a few musical gentlemen formed a club composed mainly of amateurs, but including a few professional gentlemen, prominent among whom were Charles E. Horn and son. This society was formed from three or four of our old Glee Club, and

---

* I became acquainted with Mr. Cozzens early in the beginning of the present century, and our mutual friendship continued to the end of his life. I was about two years the senior of Mr. Cozzens. In his earlier days he was a clerk in his uncle's employ. His uncle, Mr. Martlin, kept the Tammany Wigwam (then so called), on the corner of Frankfort and Spruce Streets. It was a public-house, and became prominent as being the headquarters of the Tammany Society. It was there I became intimately acquainted with him. After the death of Mr. Martlin, Mr. Cozzens succeeded to the management of the establishment. He afterwards became the proprietor of Tammany Hall, which was erected on the corner of Chatham and Frankfort Streets.

called "The Beefsteak Club." We assembled once a month, partaking of a supper in Cozzens' best style, and spending the evening in listening to songs and glees, interrupted with recitations and stories, forming altogether a most delightful evening's entertainment. We frequently had the company of the Rev. Dr. Wainwright at these sociables. I scarcely ever knew a man more extravagantly fond of music than the Doctor. If my memory serves me, these musical entertainments continued for about three years.

While at West Point, Mr. Cozzens was in the habit of visiting the city twice in the week to procure for his tables the best and greatest delicacies that our markets afforded, and it was on one of these visits that he was suddenly stricken down with apoplexy and died. Since that time his sons have continued the house, with credit to themselves and satisfaction to all their visitors.

But now comes an episode in my life, which happened at this hotel, that brings the tears to my eyes. The joy, the pride, the life and light of my heart, died there. I cannot enter into the details of her death. When I remember her, with that gentleness of character and purity of mind, (I am so sad) I feel myself unprepared to speak of her splendid qualities and attainments. I can, at times, hear her voice ringing in my ears with those melodious notes that will last with me while I exist—

> The good die first,
> But those whose hearts are like the summer dust
> Burn to the socket.

WILLIAM B. NIBLO.

Many years ago Mr. William B. Niblo kept a public-house on the corner of Pine and William Streets, where he did a profitable business. He eventually removed, and leased the property on the corner of Broadway and Prince Street for a number of years. He erected a very pretty theatre on these grounds, and, in connection with the garden he had established there, rendered it the most pleasant resort in the city. Mr. Niblo, in connection with the Ravel family, will long be remembered. This troupe drew nightly to the theatre immense audiences, and Mr. Niblo made a fortune from their engagement. This celebrated company of artistes were known throughout the length and breadth of the land. Scarcely a stranger visited the city but went to Niblo's to witness their wonderful performances. Their pantomime plays were innocent, and not only delighted and pleased the child, but the gray-headed veteran of fourscore sat entranced at their magical power. And for myself, I must say I never retired from one of their performances without having enjoyed the utmost pleasure and delight.

Some years since the Italian opera was given at Niblo's with great success by the

Sontag troupe during their visit to this city many years ago. Sontag was an artiste of the first grade, but she had seen her best days as a vocalist. This lady was celebrated for the magnificent manner in which she dressed for the stage. I recollect attending one evening at Niblo's to hear "Norma" sung by Sontag, but was somewhat disappointed. It is well known to professional artistes that the rôle of Norma requires a mezzo-soprano voice to do justice to it, whereas it was well known that Madame Sontag's voice was in the highest register of a soprano; hence she totally failed in attempting the rôle of Norma. Sontag was well qualified to sing in light opera, and give perfect satisfaction; and it is truly wonderful to my mind that a good artiste with an established reputation should be willing to run the risk of losing it by undertaking a rôle so much above her powers to perform.

Mr. Niblo retired many years ago with a large fortune. Since then he has spent much of his time and money in collecting a gallery of paintings which is said to be one of the finest in the city. With Mr. Niblo I have had a life-long acquaintance, and a more estimable gentleman I never knew.

CHAPTER XXI.

MY PERSONAL FRIEND, N. H. WOLFE.

My dear friend, Mr. Nathaniel H. Wolfe, was a man with whom I was intimately acquainted, although in our business relations we were virtually separated, his business being in the grain trade, while mine was principally in provisions. Mr. Wolfe was a gentleman whom everybody esteemed. His nature was so genial and so social that, indeed, no one could but admire him. He had some peculiarities in his intercourse with his friends that rather enhanced than deteriorated from the pleasure of his conversation. He rationally enjoyed life, and was popular with every one. He was, like myself, very fond of the opera, and was a regular attendant at the performances. He had one of the large stage-boxes at the Academy of Music, and was treasurer of that concern for several years. In later years, when I attended the opera, I took my seat in his box, when alone, by his special invitation. Mr. Wolfe was usually successful in his business transactions, and left his family in very affluent circumstances. At the time of his decease I was confined to my house by a painful disease, and was unable to attend the, funeral of my departed friend. He died regretted by all who knew him.

SUYDAM, SAGE & CO.

With the old firm of Suydam, Sage & Co. I was on the most intimate terms, and with Mr. Suydam my relations were of the most sacred and confidential nature. This house was our backer for any amount of money we might occasionally require in our large business operations, and, in return, we were their endorsers for any amount

9

they might require from time to time. The Wall Street banks required no better paper, for it was well known to the mercantile world generally, that the former house was wealthy, and that my own had established a credit scarcely inferior to other houses of established means. This confidence in each other was never betrayed by either of our houses, which continued until the withdrawal of Mr. Ferdinand Suydam from the old house of which he was the head. Our mutual friendship continued to the end of his life.

CLAGHORN & CUNNINGHAM, OF SAVANNAH.

These gentlemen, with whom I have been so long associated, deserve more than a passing notice, they being the oldest living firm on my books; and our constant intercourse has been of the most pleasant and agreeable character, which has ripened into a mutual friendship that can only cease when I am gone. The old firm was Claghorn

& Wood; they are both dead, and the son of Mr. Claghorn associated with him Mr. Cunningham. The standing and character of this firm, in its mercantile relations, ranks as high in the estimation of their fellow-citizens, for probity, honesty, and industry, as that of any house in this country.

WILLIAM P. WINCHESTER.

I cannot omit in this little history to make mention of those personal friends with whom I have been so long associated, socially as well as in mercantile transactions.

In speaking of William P. Winchester, of Boston, I am at a loss for words to convey the regard I had for him. If ever a man lived who deserved the title of "nature's nobleman" it was William P. Winchester. My relations with him in business affairs, as well as socially, leave upon my mind recollections that never can be obliterated while I exist. During our intercourse we had large transactions in business matters, and when I recall him, even now, to my memory, I often wish that many others had possessed his noble and elegant character. It was a pleasure to transact business with him, and during our large transactions, nothing ever occurred to mar the friendship and regard we mutually entertained for each other. I was frequently called to Boston on business, and although the Tremont House was my home while there, I was invariably the recipient of his hospitality. Mr. Winchester's country seat was a short distance from Boston, on the Charles River, and, truly, a princely place it was. I attended, many years ago, on the 4th of July, a *fête-champêtre* given by him at this place, and the entertainment was in keeping with the man. I never attended so elegant an affair. In less than a month after this fête was given he was carried to his vault at Mount Auburn.

" He was a man.
　Take him for all in all
　I ne'er shall look upon his like again."

JOHN SIMONDS.

With this gentleman I had large business transactions, and a more agreeable and pleasant gentleman to transact business with I never met. Our intercourse lasted for many years, and nothing ever happened to mar the feelings we mutually entertained for each other. Mr. Simonds was largely engaged in the packing of beef; his large establishment was on Lake Champlain. Our business connection lasted many years, and was profitable to both of us; and during this long connection, as before mentioned, not a jar ever disturbed the even tenor of our ways. Mr. Simonds was, in every sense, a gentleman, kind and benevolent in his nature, and a trusty friend to all who knew him. The more I became acquainted with him, the more I admired his character. Mr. Simonds died many years ago. It gives me pleasure to pay this brief tribute to his memory.

S. DAVIS, JR., & CO., OF CINCINNATI.

With this highly respectable concern, for many years past, I have done an extensive business. I was the first person who introduced their celebrated "diamond hams" into this market. I have sold many thousand tierces of them. This firm is one of the most respectable and wealthy in that city. They have done a large business with the principal dealers in the United States. I owe them many obligations for favors they have conferred on me, for which I return them my most grateful thanks.

ISAAC H. REED.

Of this gentleman, to whom I have dedicated my book, I have more than a passing word to say. I became acquainted with Mr. Reed many years ago, and our intercourse has been such that warrants me in saying I have never met a more perfect and dignified gentleman.

I have watched the career of this gentleman almost from his boyhood, and the character and culture he possesses entitle him to the respect of every one.

I have dedicated this book to him (with his permission), appreciating as I do the high sense of his character.

DR. ANDREWS.

Since my residing at the Washington Hotel, I have become intimately acquainted with Dr. Andrews, who has been a boarder at this hotel for twenty-five years, and during my sickness of the last few months he has been my daily attending physician, and a more agreeable and courteous gentleman I have never met; in short, we have become most intimate friends. The doctor is rated among our ablest physicians. He has an established reputation, and I esteem it a privilege to have made his acquaintance. I have every faith in his skill, and trust he may long live to be a benefit and blessing to his fellow-men.

JAMES LENOX.

I now wish to speak of one of the greatest philanthropists of the age. I allude to Mr. James Lenox, the only son of Robert Lenox, deceased. I was intimately acquainted with Mr. Robert Lenox, and had business transactions with him for a number of years, but I have never met his son. Notwithstanding that I never had the pleasure of his acquaintance, his wide-world reputation as a Christian philanthropist has been as familiar to my ears as if I had personally known him for years. I have been told that for many years past he has given away his annual income from his large estate, principally to the Presbyterian Church, of which he is a member, and to the charitable institutions connected there-

with, as well as to other objects of charity.
He is at the present time president of the
American Bible Society, and has been for
many years the ruling elder in the Presbyterian Church, corner of Twelfth Street
and Fifth Avenue, of which the Rev. Dr.
Paxon is pastor, formerly the Rev. Dr.
Phillips. Mr. Lenox is now completing a
splendid monument to his own memory,
namely—the Lenox Library. It is situated
on Fifth Avenue, opposite Central Park,
and occupies the entire front of one block,
and is the most massive built building in
this city, being entirely fire-proof. This
building will carry his name and Christian
liberality down to many future generations.
He has been for many years accumulating
a large library, and it is said he has now
more editions of the Bible, in different languages, than any other library in this country; and there is no doubt, when his library
is opened to the public, it will be found to
contain many of the most celebrated productions of the world.

CHAPTER XXII.

OLD LANDMARKS.—BURNHAM'S.

IN the olden times Burnham's was the celebrated stopping-place when driving out on the old Bloomingdale Road. Of a fine afternoon in summer or winter, his horse-sheds surrounding the house were filled with the fashionable equipages of the day. In the rear grounds there were magnificent views of the river. As a general rule, Burnham's was considered the end of a drive out of the city. But what has time done? This very spot that was devoted, in years gone by, to those social enjoyments, exists no longer. The rapid strides our city has made within the past twenty-five years, has broken the charms of these old landmarks. This very spot (Burnham's) that had attractions in my middle life, is now no more. Brick and brown-. stone have taken the place it once occupied.

AN EXPLANATION.

September 4th.—In casting over the various subjects treated on in these papers, including something of my history, in connection with recollections and events that have transpired in this city from 1798 to 1832, I am well aware there are many events that have occurred during this period that have escaped my recollection; but what I have written are truthful statements, and what I have said has been done to the best of my ability, and in language so plain that a child can read it. Be this as it may, I have no apology to offer for its composition, for in the very commencement of these papers I positively disclaimed any pretension to literary merit, but it is just what I intended it to be—a plain statement of plain facts. I have

many and long-tried friends in this city
who will overlook the many faults which
this book contains. These papers were
commenced the first of last March, (1874,)
and have been continued from day to day,
with the exception only when I felt unwell
and disqualified to proceed with them; for
there are times when the mind wanders
from its subject, in which case it is impos-
sible to write satisfactorily. Then, again,
an inspiration will flash across the mind,
and you can then convey your thoughts
with ease and pleasure, without racking the
brain to convey it in language just suited
to the occasion. I beg here to remark that,
previous to my commencing these papers,
all my previous writings were with my
business correspondents, and private letters to my relatives and friends. I had
neither time nor disposition for any other
writing. It only occurred to me seven
months ago of writing a short history, and
that idea was only thought of as giving my

mind employment, for my business had nearly left me nothing to do,—and I must be busy about something.

I beg here to remark that I have been very much afflicted with a most painful complaint during the writing of these papers, not debarring me from visiting the Exchange and my office, but rendering me unable to attend church on Sundays, which is a great misfortune for me, having been brought up from my early boyhood in its teachings. I became very much attached to its Christian institutions, and a firm believer in its doctrines; but my Sundays now are all passed at home. In several of my earlier papers I gave some interesting accounts of the Italian Opera in this city, for I was a most enthusiastic admirer and supporter of that favorite amusement, which I always considered a moral one; but my present age and infirmities prevent me from attending any more on its fascinating enjoyments.

BROADWAY AND GRAND STREET.

On the north-east corner of Broadway and Grand Street, where now stands the immense store formerly occupied by Brooks Brothers, stood a large-sized wooden building, some seventy years ago, occupied as a house of entertainment, and in the rear was a high hill or sand-bank that extended to the East River. Immediately in the rear of the house, and on this hill, was an enclosure fitted with seats and boxes for the accommodation of the patrons of the house. This place was called "Bunker Hill," as it was on a level with the second or third story of the house. On a Sunday afternoon or a holiday, a set of boys, or half-grown men, myself among the number, would resort there to drink "Mead." The house became very celebrated for this delightful beverage. I have frequently thought that this simple drink has been the cause of saving many men from destruction. I have not seen a bottle of this "mead" for many years, and have often wondered at its banishment from general use. The old Broadway House was used, in former years, as a gathering-place for the politicians of our city, and when nominations were made for future elections. There are many associations connected with this house as a rendezvous for other purposes than politics. There were frequent advertisements in the daily papers for meetings there for various objects, which my memory of fifty or sixty years ago fails me to particularize.

WASHINGTON HOTEL, NO. 1 BROADWAY.

Myself and daughter are now boarders at this hotel, where we have been, at the present writing, some fourteen months; and I shall probably remain here during the remainder of my life, for I am better suited and accommodated than I have been at any time since I broke up housekeeping.

My landlord, Mr. Dingley, is a very pleasant and agreeable gentleman, and does all in his power to please his boarders. His tables are well supplied with all the varieties of the season, hence I am perfectly satisfied. Mr. Dingley is an Eastern man, and has a large number of friends who patronize his house. He is doing a prosperous business, and I consider him justly entitled to success by his prompt attention to his business, as well as promoting the comfort of his guests. The main house, on the corner, was the private residence of Mr. Nathaniel Prime, the senior partner of the old firm of Prime, Ward, King & Co. This building when erected, over one hundred years ago, was the most noted private dwelling in this city. The ceilings in the parlors are as lofty as those of many of the most fashionable houses of the present day. The marble mantels were imported from Europe, and the large mirrors in the parlors are as large and lofty as those we meet with in our first-class residences. The location of this house is certainly very beautiful, taking in the whole range of the Battery and the harbor. A more delightful spot cannot be found in this city.

TRINITY CHIMES.

July 13th.—The Trinity chimes this morning advise me this is Sunday. These chimes I have been in the habit of listening to for the past seventy-five years. They are doubtless the best bells in this country, and are usually played by first-class artistes; but it is melancholy to reflect on the number of death-knells they have sounded during the past seventy-five years. A few more short years or days of pleasure or pain will consign the present generation to their final resting-place, and God grant it may prove to be to a blessed immortality beyond the grave!

CHAPTER XXIII.

BROOKLYN.

AUGUST 31, 1874.—It was not until this morning, in casting my mind over for a subject to note down in this history, that I observed Brooklyn had escaped my recollection, and strange to say, Brooklyn, in 1798, did not contain one hundred houses from the Navy Yard to the South Ferry. It has now a population of over half a million of souls; and, in honesty, I feel bound to acknowledge my almost utter ignorance of its history, almost as much so as if I should undertake to give a history of London or Liverpool, which I never saw. Brooklyn is located on the Island of my birth, but I undertake to say that the farthest I have travelled back in Brooklyn during

the past twenty-five years was to Green-
wood Cemetery. In my youthful days,
when I was, say from seventeen to twenty
years of age, I was in the habit, with com-
panions of my own age, of occasionally
visiting Brooklyn, of a Sunday afternoon,
and walking up from the ferry, about a
mile and a half, to the sign of the "Black
Horse," a house of entertainment for man
and beast, for the sole purpose of partaking of my favorite beverage "mead."

HOBOKEN.

It is at least twenty-five years since I have
visited Hoboken. In former days I was a
frequent visitor there, and there are many
pleasing recollections associated with the
place that render it interesting to me. The
Elysian Fields and surroundings was a spot
made classic by Halleck the poet. It was,
in former days, selected by the duellists as
the ground on which to settle their quarrels.
It was the spot where Aaron Burr shot

Hamilton; it was on these grounds that the son of the latter was killed by his antagonist; the name of the latter I disremember, but with whom I was previously acquainted. To return to more pleasing recollections, it was the ground on which the old Green Turtle Club held their semi-annual gatherings, which Mr. Talman presided over, and superintended the preparations of the feast. It was pleasant to wander among these delightful walks; in fact, Hoboken as it was some thirty years ago, was one of the most pleasant rambling places in the vicinity of our city.

CHAPTER XXIV.

THE PAPERS I SUBSCRIBE TO.

I HAVE been, for a very long time, a sub-scriber to the *New York Observer* and the *Home Journal,* both weekly papers, also to the evening *Commercial Advertiser.* This paper I have taken for over fifty years. My old friend, Colonel Stone, was the senior editor many years ago. I have always esteemed the *Commercial* as the most reli-able of all our evening papers; I take great pleasure in having it read to me. The *Observer* is another one of my life-long papers; as a religious sheet there is noth-ing in this country that can approach it. It is conducted by gentlemen of marked ability, and has had an immense circula-tion throughout the country for years.

The letters of "Irenæus" are perfect models in their way, and to me it is a perfect delight to read them. As before remarked, I have taken the *Home Journal* since it was first established. It is a delightful paper for light reading; it gives its readers all the fashionable news of the day, and, taken altogether, is a very enjoyable and interesting journal.

THE "LEDGER."

In regard to my early education, I would here remark that the schools of eighty years ago were very inferior. The common routine of studies were reading, spelling, writing and arithmetic, and even these were very imperfectly taught. I lay no claim to literary merit, but I was always very fond of reading, and that fondness still absorbs my leisure hours; and, as my eyesight fails me in my old age, one of my daughters reads to me nightly. My favorite poetic authors are Fitz-Greene Halleck,

Sir Walter Scott, Wordsworth, Pope, and Cowper, and many others I might mention that I am not so familiar with. In these rambling sketches I use the best and plainest language I am capable of, and although my diction is at fault in many instances, I know my old friends and acquaintances will relish their perusal, notwithstanding that want of polish and diction which so charms the reader.

I have taken the *New York Ledger* since its first introduction, and I esteem it one of the best literary papers published in this country that I have any knowledge of. The writers and correspondents of this paper are of the highest order, and Mr. Bonner, the editor, is doubtless very proud of them, although, it is said, he pays them more money for their productions than any other weekly paper in the United States. Of course I have my own favorites; John G. Saxe, the poetical contributor, is a great favorite of mine. Sylvanus Cobb, Mrs. Southworth, and Mrs. Harriet Lewis are my especial favorites in the long continued stories. In the single articles, the Rev. Henry Ward Beecher, Rev. Dr. Hall, Judge Clark, and James Parton. All these correspondents are very able writers, and three or four of them stand decidedly at the head of their profession. The lady writers of single articles are usually very good and interesting; but the *Ledger* lost a great favorite in Fanny Fern. Her articles were so terse and witty they commanded the universal admiration of all its readers. I will now allude to Professor Leon Lewis. His stories are so fiendishly tragic, as a general thing, that I cannot fail to believe but that they are manufactured out of a feverish brain. The characters he portrays are totally inconsistent with the general rules that govern even outlaws and bravados; in a word, his characters are overdrawn, and I am free to confess I take very little pleasure in their perusal. Far be it from

me to deteriorate from his literary acquire-
ments and character as a writer, for those
are of the first order; and were he to deal
with less brutal and inhuman characters he
would be generally read with much more
pleasure and satisfaction. There are many
beautiful and even brilliant passages in
many of his stories that atone, in some
measure, for the other characters which he
represents. I have no pretension as a critic,
and the observations I have made on the
writers of the *Ledger* are my own, and may
be taken by the public for what they are
worth.

CHAPTER XXV

THE THEATRE.

In 1798, when my father removed to this city, there was but one theatre—the old Park. Mr. Simpson was for a long time the manager, and was, by the by, a very excellent and popular comedian. And while on this subject I desire to say that I have not seen or attended a play for the past thirty-five years of my life, with the exception of once. Some years ago I was prevailed upon by an old friend who was visiting me, to accompany him to Wallack's, to witness a celebrated comedy. I did so, and was delighted.

In my early days I frequently visited the theatre, and saw all the celebrated actors and actresses of the day. Fanny

Kemble probably created as great an enthusiasm as any actress of those days. It was not until the advent of Malibran, in Italian opera, that I lost all taste for plays—for my very soul was wrapped in music—and all theatrical performances were of but little interest to me.

Alas! Alas! old age, with some of its infirmities, are crowding on me, and the recollections of the pleasures and enjoyments of my earlier years are passing swiftly away, and it is now only in the dim retrospect of the past that I can now and then discover a bright star of hope that points to a blessed immortality beyond the grave.

RECREATION.

July 14th.—We are now in the middle of summer, when it is generally supposed the more fashionable portion of our citizens are on the wing visiting the various fashionable resorts for recreation and pleasure; and, indeed, they must be fastidious if they cannot find some spot for enjoyment. As I have before remarked, for thirty-five years of my life I was in the habit of visiting, with my family, all the principal re sorts that abound at the north, and I can say, with truth, that it was always a season of pleasure and enjoyment both to myself and family, and better prepared me for my active business in the future. But my time for those pleasures have passed away forever. Ninety years now confine me at home, and increasing debility inclines me to quiet and repose.

CHAPTER XXVI.

MY BUST ON THE EXCHANGE.

MANY years ago a few of my old friends waited upon me, and requested me (if I had no objections) to sit for my "bust," to be placed on the Exchange, in Wall Street. I assented to their wishes, and the "bust" was executed by a Mr. Jones, who, as I understand, is now dead. The following correspondence will explain itself :—

To ABRAM S. JEWELL, ESQ.,
        President of the New York Produce
            Exchange.

Dear Sir,—About twenty years ago I was waited upon by several of my friends in the produce business, requesting me to "sit" to a sculptor to have my "bust" modeled in clay, to which I consented. After it was finished there were some twenty or thirty "casts" of it modeled in plaster of Paris, which the sculptor sold for his own benefit at ten dollars each. My friends then concluded to have one executed in marble, which was accordingly done. The cost of the original in clay was one hundred dollars, and the marble one four hundred dollars. The marble "bust" was on exhibition at the Exchange (now the Custom House) about one year. The Exchange removed to the corner of Broad and South Streets, where it remained another year, when a committee of three or the subscribers came and presented it to me for my own personal use. I then took it to my residence, where it has remained until the present time. And here I beg leave to say that I am to this day ignorant of the names of many of those who subscribed towards the payment of this "bust." To them I tender my warm and heartfelt thanks, and fully appreciate the honor conferred upon me. In my will, made many years ago, I bequeathed this "bust" to the President and Directors of the New York Produce Exchange; but I have recently made up my mind, in consequence of my removal shortly from my present abode, to send my "bust" to your Produce Exchange while I am still alive, provided you deem it worthy of a niche in some corner of your Exchange.

Truly yours,

(Signed)   N. T. HUBBARD.

NEW YORK, July 30, 1872.

NEW YORK PRODUCE EXCHANGE,
NEW YORK, August 2, 1872.

N. T. HUBBARD, ESQ.

Sir,—I have the honor to acknowledge receipt of yours of the 30th ultimo, addressed to the President of the New York Produce Exchange, kindly offering to anticipate a bequest made by you, many years ago, of your marble bust, to the President and Directors of the New York Produce Exchange.

By action of the Board, the generous offer made by you was accepted, and the Secretary was instructed to return to you the thanks of the Board for the same, with their hearty wishes for the extension and happiness of your already long and eventful life. In behalf of the President and Board of Managers,

I am, very respectfully, &c.,

(Signed)   J. E. HULSHIZER, *Secretary.*

CHAPTER XXVII.

MY GOLDEN WEDDING.

NOVEMBER 9th, 1861, we celebrated our golden wedding at my old residence on Washington Square, surrounded by all my children and a large number of grand-children. What a pleasant reminiscence to recur to, that I should have celebrated this great event, for how few ever attain to it! It was my pleasure and pride, on that evening, to stand beside one, after fifty years of married life of uninterrupted happiness and prosperity, and to look upon her with the same love and affection that bound us together for that great length of time. It was certainly a delightful occasion, and a pleasant reunion of dear relatives and friends, several of whom were present at

our *first wedding*. It seemed almost like
a dream to realize that those fifty years
had flown so quickly by; but many who
were then present have since passed away,
both old and young, while I, the oldest of
the assemblage, still linger on the earth.
But great changes have come over my life
since then—the loss of dear loved ones
and loss of property; but as God has willed
it so let me be resigned. My Heavenly
Father knows what is best for us all. My
children and friends were lavish in their
tokens of love and affection, and I shall
ever remember the kindly regards that
were shown on that occasion. May the
noble virtues of that loved wife and mother
be instilled into the minds of those children
still living, and their end shall be peace.

My dear wife died seven years after
this event, on the 4th of February, 1868,
mourned and regretted by all who knew
her.

In Memoriam.

JULIA AUGUSTA.

August 31st, 1874.—This is the anniversary of the death of my beloved daughter —the musical bird of my family. She died suddenly, of congestion of the brain, at Cozzens's Hotel, West Point, where my family had been stopping for some five or six weeks. We were preparing to leave for home the day she died. The loss of this daughter, at so early an age (she was but twenty-one), with that magnificent voice, combined with a disposition that lent all the graces and virtues to womanhood, causes me to mourn to this day her loss.

> " None knew her but to love her,
> None named her but to praise."

My daughter left an infant son (nine months old) at her death, Francis H. Saltus, Jr. He is now grown to manhood, and is a young man of superior talents, has been educated mostly in Europe, is a great linguist, speaking five or six different languages, and inherits, in a degree, the musical talent of his mother. He has composed several very beautiful pieces of music, and it has often given me great pleasure to listen to his performances.

CHAPTER XXVIII.

PARSON GREENE.

BEFORE closing these papers I cannot re frain from quoting, from my "Uncle Grif fin's Biographical Sketches," a most inter- esting account of Zachariah Greene, then known on Long Island as "Parson Greene." He took an important part in our Revolu- tionary struggle, and the character of the man (as told by Mr. Griffin) has so often struck me that I deem it not improper to repeat it in these papers.

―――――

"'Parson Greene' is the familiar name by which our hero is known and distinguished from all other men throughout the length and breadth of Long Island. He is the

only parson in Hempstead, at least; all
the other parsons are only ministers.   In
many respects Goldsmith's description of
the 'Vicar of Wakefield' portrays the person and accomplishments of Parson Greene.
Perhaps the Vicar's habits of contentment
never reached the same happy summit as is
realized in our own parson.   The parson is
the more interesting, as he is a living book
—all fact and no fiction: he can be read
in conversation.   He speaks of sermons in
the pulpit, and battles in the Revolutionary struggle, with like affability and ease.
He listens with his left ear, but looks pene-
tratingly with both eyes, while he speaks
fluently, with the affectionate authority of
a father, and commends everything he says
to the sons, and particularly to the daughters of his hearers.   He looks hale, plump
and hearty, and always says he is well.
He is the happiest man on Long Island.
He entertains the prospect of death with
the same pleasure as the reception of a

friend. In short, he is the gentleman, the scholar, the patriot, and the Christian.

"At the age of sixteen years, just at the time of his leaving school, the cause of his country called him from private life, and with a beloved brother he entered the army under Captain Amos Walbridge, in Colonel Reed's regiment, Brigadier Glover's brigade, and joined it at Roxbury. General Washington was Commander-in-Chief, and headed an army of men who were soldiers from patriotic motives—men determined to have a place in national representation as well as national taxation—men whose souls had been tried by the tyranny of kings and the petty despotism of kings' courtiers. It was under these circumstances that Zachariah Greene entered the ranks of the Revolutionary army under Washington, and for these reasons he fought in its battles.

"He aided in the erection of the fort at Dorchester, which was commenced one

evening at sundown, and at sunrise next
morning his party had cannon playing
upon Boston, and succeeded in driving
the British out of Boston, from whence
they sailed down the bay to Castle William. Here they run ashore and burned all
the buildings on Dorchester Neck. They
cannonaded the Neck the whole night, with
grapeshot and chainshot, firing over the
American troops, ultimately succeeding in
destroying a poor man's orchard. He
moved, with the army under Washington,
from Roxbury to New York, and landed
there in April, where he aided in the erection of the fort on Brooklyn Heights. He
left New York with the army when it
evacuated, and went above Kingsbridge.

" When the British arrived at Throgg's
Point the battle commenced, and lasted till
the armies were separated by the messenger
of the great arbiter—Darkness. Soon
after this he was in the battle of White
Plains, in 1776. In 1777 the same com-

pany was joined to Captain Webb's company in Connecticut. He was with the party which was sent to take the fort at Brookhaven, which was built round the Presbyterian church, of which, twenty-one years after, he was installed pastor. He was in the body of men who marched into the region of Philadelphia, and was at the battle of White Marsh. During the engagement he received a wound in the left shoulder, on the 7th of September, 1777, his shoulder-blade being shattered. It was three days before he had any attention paid to his wound; at the end of which time he applied to Dr. Robinson, a surgeon, who had been taken prisoner, to attend to his wants. He told Dr. R. that he would compensate him. Dr. R. asked him if he was not afraid to trust an enemy. He replied, 'I can trust a gentleman.' Dr. R. attended to his case, and succeeded in healing up the wound. Mr. Greene put his right-hand, containing the compensation, behind his back, and told the doctor to shake hands with him in that attitude. The doctor thanked him, and expressed a great desire to have his wife and children on this side of the Atlantic, saying if they were here he should stay altogether.

"The above is the result of Mr. Greene's experience as stated by himself. Being of little more service in the army, as he was no longer able to bear arms, at the request of his father, and by order of General Washington, he was discharged from the army, having, with a good patriotic heart and manly soul aided the cause of his country in several of its hardest battles.

"During the winter of 1780, in the month of January, he walked sixteen miles on a pair of snow-shoes for the purpose of securing a small Latin book, which he required to aid him in his preparation for college. He had now entered, according to his own words, 'an army in which he was determined to fight for a better De-

claration of Independence than the last.'
He resolved to be a soldier of Christ.

"In the year 1782 he entered Dartmouth
College, but had been engaged in study but
a short time when, owing to bad health,
he was compelled, for a season, to withdraw. After a considerable recess, he as-
sumed the cares of a student once more.
He subsequently studied theology with
Amzi Lewis, of Orange County, New
York.

"Having passed through all the preliminary and initiatory steps necessary to pre-
pare him for the ministry, he was duly
licensed to preach on the first day of February, 1785. In the year 1800 he visited the
scene of his collegiate experience at Dartmouth, and upon his return the faculty of
that institution honored him with a diploma,
which he has prized very highly through
life. From the time of his ordination, till
within the last few years, he has labored
'in season and out of season' in the minis-

try, pursuing an even course, and doing much good to his fellow-men in all the realities of life. During this period of service he endeavored to increase the happiness of two thousand individuals, by uniting them (one thousand couples) in the 'holy bands of matrimony.'"

———

In connection with the foregoing extract, I desire to say that, when quite a lad, I frequently heard Parson Greene preach at the church at Catchogue, where he was settled on the 27th of September, 1797.

APPENDIX.

[ALLUSION has been made by Mr. Hubbard in the foregoing narrative to some of the circumstances attending the execution of the marble bust of himself which now occupies a prominent place in the Produce Exchange, but the following additional facts, kindly contributed by one of the original subscribers to that fine work of art, will have especial interest as the voluntary testimony of one who has long enjoyed a familiar acquaintance with the subject of this memoir.]

NEW YORK, March 18, 1875.

IT is seldom that the active life of a busy merchant is prolonged to the extent of that of our friend and neighbor, Mr. NATHANIEL T. HUBBARD. Having been personally acquainted with him, and intimate in his family, since 1824 (now fifty-one years), it seems proper that I should, as an appendage to this book containing the reminiscences of a man who has for so long a period maintained an unblemished character for mercantile probity and honor, give a history of the *marble bust* which now adorns the rooms of the Produce Exchange.

In 1855, through the exertions of Mr. Theodore Johnson, of the firm of Seguine & Johnsons (who had formerly been a clerk with Mr. Hubbard), assisted by myself, we secured the services of T. D. Jones, the sculptor, and procured a subscription of fifty names, at ten dollars each, myself and Mr. Todd, the salt merchant, being the only persons outside of the regular provision business. In behalf of the subscribers, I was deputed to present the bust, which service I performed on New Year's day, 1856. It was not given to a Hero, Politician, or Author, but was the spontaneous offering of friends to a man who had, in his endeavors to maintain the highest standard of mercantile integrity, become entitled to their respect and honor. The following correspondence took place on the occasion.

E. BILL.

NEW YORK, January 1, 1856.

N. T. HUBBARD, Esq.:

Dear Sir—A few of your personal friends, appreciating your character, and feeling disposed to present you with some solid testimonial thereof, secured the services of T. D. Jones, an eminent American sculptor, for the purpose of procuring your *bust* in *marble*. That artist has faithfully performed his task, and given us a most truthful representation of one whom we take pleasure in thus honoring. Our object has been, not only to hand down to posterity the features of an *old friend*, but to evince our appreciation of that character for *sterling honesty* which has always characterized your dealings, and made the adage so applicable to yourself, "His *word* is as good as his *bond*." In asking your acceptance of this testimonial, which we now do, we beg to convey with it our best wishes for your health and happiness.

In behalf of the subscribers, and with many good wishes personally,

I am truly yours,

EDWARD BILL.

NEW YORK, January 7, 1856.

EDWARD BILL, Esq.,
        on behalf of the subscribers, etc. :

Dear Sir—Your communication of the 1st inst. was duly received, accompanied by the presentation of a marble bust, executed by T. D. Jones, Esq., of this city. For this testimonial of your esteem I tender those who have procured its execution my most heartfelt thanks, and I assure you that it is the richest gift you could bestow, as it is the most valuable legacy my children can receive.

This compliment is doubly enhanced from the circumstance that it is received from gentlemen who, for a long time, have been engaged in the same branch of business as myself; and to have secured the respect of those with whom I have had almost daily intercourse for years is a gratification and pleasure which I have not words to express.

With sentiments of esteem and respect, please accept my best wishes for your future prosperity and happiness.

N. T. HUBBARD.

SUBSCRIBERS' NAMES.

It having become known to some of Mr. Hubbard's intimate friends on the New York Produce Exchange that he had prepared a sketch of his life, with a view to publication, they organized a committee, consisting of Messrs. Abraham S. Jewell, Charles H. Johnson, J. E. Hulshizer, Charles W. Strachan, James R. Turner, Archibald Harris, and Frank Kimball, to take charge of the publication, and relieve Mr. Hubbard from all care and risk in the matter, which they were enabled to do through the following subscribers.

The work of carrying the volume through the press was entrusted to Mr. Grant, Superintendent of the Exchange, who kindly gave the matter his personal supervision.

New York, *March* 31, 1875.

ABBOTT, J. H.
ACKERMAN, C. T.
ATWATER, T. S.
ALLEN, F. H.
AMELUNG, HENRY.
ANDERSON, J.
ALEXANDER, JAS. A.
ANNAN, E.
ALBERT, F. P.
ARMOUR, PLANKINTON & Co.
ARCHER, Jr., D. O.
ARCHBOLD, J. D.

BAXTER & Co., ARCHIBALD.
BILL, EDWARD.
BENSON, R. H.
BALDWIN, JAS. L.
BOGERT, B. C.
BURKHOLDER & MCCUTCHEN.
BOND, JNO. H.
BURT, HAYES & Co.
BOSTWICK, J. B.
BOUCK, JAS. B.
BECHTEL, Jr., G. J.
BREWSTER, J. L.
BARTLETT, G. A.
BRUSH, W. F.
BREWSTER, A. H.
BARRETTO, G. M.
BARBER, W. B.
BUTLER, E. M.
BURT, J. M.
BINGHAM, DAVID.
BONNELL, A.
BEYER, JOHN A.
BROOKER, J. P.
BOWLER, GEO. T.
BAXTER, WARREN C.
BLOOM, W. J.
BOWNES, JOS. W.
BURGESS, E. G.
BARKLEY, JOHN F.
BENNETT, C. E.
BESTER, R. S.
BOSTWICK, J. A.
BUSHNELL, THOS. C.

CHAMBERLIN, J. M.
CHASE, THEO. B.
CRAMER, J. L.
COBB, S. R.
CONNELL, D.

CRAMER, L. V.
CLOSE, JOHN W.
COLGATE, SAMUEL.
CHAMBERS, H. F. S.
CHAMBERLIN, ROE & Co.
CHAMBERS, G. F.
COOPER, JOHN B.
CLARK, M. E.
CARLL, S. S.
CECIL, Jr., GEO.
COLEMAN & Co., E. W.
CONKLIN, JOHN S.
CHURCHMAN, ALFRED.
COLE, W. A.
COBB, E. H. & SON.
CRANE, MUNROE.
COOK BROS. & MCCORD.
CAMERDEN, JNO.

DOWS & Co., DAVID.
DALLY, SAMUEL.
DANIELS, H. L.
DOYLE, JAMES.
DAVIS, L.
DOUGLASS, R. J.
DOUGHERTY, JOHN.
DECKER, S. C.
DOUGHERTY, E. H.
DUNN, SAMUEL P.
DUSENBERY, HENRY.
DEWOLF, D. R.
DENSLOW & BUSH.

ELLSWORTH, J. W.
EDSON, FRANKLIN.
ELLIS, THOMAS.
ELLIOTT, A. W.
EMMENS, G. W.

FACKINER, JNO.
FOWLER BROS.
FULLER, WM. H.
FLOYD, BENJ. W.
FINK, VALENTINE.
FROST, I. T.
FISKE & Co., J. M.
FOX, W. H.
FERRIS & Co., GEO. B.
FLINT, JAS. L.
FOSTER, C. G.
FORD, S. R.
FERRIS, J. J.

FREDERICK, N.
FENBY, JOS. B.
FEIGELSTOCK, A.
FLEISCHMANN, MAX.
FORCE, S. C.

GORMAN & CO.
GRIGGS, D. A.
GARDNER, A. V.
GILLETT, M. H.
GOODEVE, JAS.
GOULARD, THOS.
GOPSILL, THOS. M.
GODWIN, JOS.
GRANT, S. H.

HULSHIZER, J. E.
HOLMAN, L. F.
HAZELTINE, L.
HAZELTINE, J. M.
HEUBERER, C. E.
HARRIS, W. H.
HEBERT, HENRY B.
HEBERT, JOHN H.
HARRISON, S. D.
HOWE, E. T.
HARRISON, THOS. D.
HALSTEAD, P. S.
HIBBARD, L. D.
HIGGINS, W. B.
HAUCK, J.
HARRIS, T. R.
HICKS, H. E.
HYATT & MOUNT.
HARRIS, ARCH.
HENEY, A. T.
HINCKEN, EDW.
HOLT & CO.
HOLMES, A. L.
HEYE, GUSTAV.

IVES, EDWARD.
INGERSOLL, HORACE.

JONES, JACOB.
JEWELL, H. S.
JACOBY, S.
JOHNSON, G. F. & CO.
JEWELL, A. S.
JEWELL, EBEN M.
JOHNSON, E. A.
JONES, A. A.

JOHNSON, C. H.
JONES, GEO. I.
JEWELL, JOHN V.
JEFFREY, G. M.
JEWELL, EDWARD M.
JARVIS, JAS. L.

KELLER, FRED.
KNOWLES, S. W.
KINGAN & CO.
KENT, E. A.
KNAPP, MILTON.
KNAPP, GEO. C.
KEENEY, GEO. M.
KIMBALL, C. A.
KENDALL, WM.

LAIMBEER, R. H.
LOCKWOOD, C. B.
LOGAN, JAMES.
LEGGETT, R. L.
LEWIS, EDW'D J.
LEA, RICHARD M.
LAMSON, E. O.
LOSEE, FRANCIS.
LOWE, JOHN
LOUNSBERY, JAS. H.

McEWAN, JAS. W.
MACFARLANE, V. W.
MOSES, A.
MILLSPAUGH, P. M.
MEDAY, C. H.
MARVIN, W. T.
McILVAINE, A. E.
MOSES, WM.
MONTGOMERY, ARCH.
MEDAY, GEO. K.
MANWARING, WM. M.
MILLER, HIRAM.
McEWEN, GEO. C.
MANWARING, JR., D. W.
MANGAM, D. D.
McCORD, H. D.
MYERS, M. C.
METTLER, JR., S.
MANGAM, E. B.
McTAVISH, D. A.
MOORE, EDW'D A.
MANWARING, D. W
MYERS, MASON
MILLER, J. T.

MACY, Jr., JOSIAH.
McGEE, JAS.
MEISSNER, FRED.

N. Y. PRODUCE EXCHANGE.
NASH, THOS. C.
NEWLIN, EDW'D.

PARKER, C.
PARKER, F. H.
PATRICK, ROBT.
PRESTON, WM. I.
POWER, WM. H.
PAXSON, WM.
PHILLIPS & CO.
POPHAM, WM. H.
PARTRICK, GEO. F.
POWELL, Jr., WM.
PAULES, JOHN H.
PARKER, CHAS. F.
PAYNE, WM. H.
PEEK, P. F.
POTTER, J. W.
PATTERSON, CLAPP & CO.
PHINNEY, E. S.
PARKINSON, ROBERT.
POUCH, A. J.

ROBERTS, WM. P.
RICE, L. J.
RANDOLPH, T. E. F.
ROBBINS, S. T.
ROGERS, G.
ROMER, ALFRED.
RICH, C. E.
ROUNDEY, B. B.
ROUSE, MARTIN.
REED, HORATIO.
REED, H. M.
ROOD, L. W.
ROHE, CHAS.
REED & CO., I. H.
ROBERTS, A. F.
RICE, E. C.
ROBERSON, S.
RYDER, S. O.
ROBB, J. W.
ROGERS, H. C.
ROCKEFELLER, WM.

SPRING, A.
SINCLAIR & CO., JNO.

STRUBLE, ISAAC J.
SINCLAIR, A.
STRACHAN, CHAS. W.
STEVENS, ASA.
STUTZER, HERMAN.
SMITH, W. J.
SPEAR, CHARLES.
SMITH, H. W.
STEARS, W. L. B.
SMITH & CO., F. E.
SPAULDING, A. S.
SANFORD, CARL.
SIMONS, A. H.
SMITH, CORNELIUS.
SQUIRES, A. L.
SCHOONMAKER, L. H.
STONE, GEO. C.
SMITH & CO., GEO.
SKIDMORE, C. H.
SILBERHORN, W. H.
STORY, W. H.
SHOTWELL, H. W.
SHOTWELL, THEO.
SERGEANT, A. J.
SUYDAM, WALTER L.
STENSON, SAMUEL.
SHAFER, N. B.
STEPHENSON, FRED.
SCHEDLER & CO., F. X.
SEAGER, J. C.

TRAVIS, W. S.
TEFFT, P. C.
TALLMAN, J. H.
TRIPP & KETCHAM.
TOBEY, JNO. A.
TRIGG, GEO P.
TURNER, JAS. R.
THOMAS, W. W.
TOMPKINS, H. W.
TONJES, CHAS. F.
THOMAS, EVAN.
THORNE, J. W.
TOBEY & BOOTH.
TITUS, EDMUND.
TRENCH, JOHN.
THALLON, ROBT.

VAN WAGONER, P. H.
VAN TASSEL, E. M.
VOORHEES, W. K.
VAIL, D. S.

Van Wagenen, C. D.
Van Tassel, J. A.
Vatable, H. A.
Valentine, Stephen.

Work, W. A.
Watts & Mathews.
Woodbury, F. P.
Walker, James.
Webb, Henry.
Woolsey, T. B.
Wright & Byrne.
Whitman, E. S.
Wolfe, N. H.
Wilcox & Co., W. J.
Ward, J. S.

Williams & Co., H.
Williams, W.
Welch, P. A.
Ward, H. C.
Wynkoop, Jas. D.
Williamson, Wm.
Whitlock, Geo.
Walker, E. H.
Warner, A.
Weeks, Forster J.

Yellowlee, R. A.
Young, J. S.
Yale, Amerton.
Yeomans, S. A.

www.ingramcontent.com/pod-product-compliance
Lightning Source LLC
Chambersburg PA
CBHW030642030726
47497CB00006B/1908